THE BOX

Bryan Kollar

Bryan Kollar

Acknowledgements and Shout Outs

Shout outs and thank yous go to the following:

- All the artists who allowed me to use their artwork throughout this book. I have given credit to every artist under each photo.
  You can find JellyEmily on her Facebook page: https://www.facebook.com/jellyemily
- Thank you again to every single character in this book who let me use your real first and last names. Just like my other three books, I either know you, have met you, or have talked to you in some way or another through social medial. I do hope you all like the part I have chosen for you.
- Thank you to the two businesses who let me use their company name in my book:
  1. Elio Motors – the futuristic looking vehicle that exists today. Visit their website at www.ElioMotors.com
  2. Lanes Cranes – Visit their website at www.LanesCraneService.com

Since every character in this book is a real person, it would only make sense to have real business names too.

Original cover art by Alicia Hope
http://www.aliciahopeauthor.blogspot.com

The Box

Blurb

In order to travel back in time and accomplish a secret mission, Blake Stone builds the world's first time travel device, The Box. That's great, you say? Sure. Except that on its first back-in-time 'road-test', The Box accidentally takes him 329 years into the future to the year 2345!

What the—?

No biggie, you say, he can use The Box to go back. Sure … except it was damaged in transit. And as the 'out-dated' parts needed to repair his only means of transport don't exist in 2345, Blake finds himself stranded in a strange time and place with no way home.

THE BOX

CHAPTER 1

"This is too cliché, Dad."

Blake pushed several buttons to display a specific pattern of multi-colored lights. "Don't worry. I'll paint it. It'll look nothing like a telephone booth, I promise."

"But no matter how you paint it, it's still going to look like one."

"Then I'll move the electronics into something else."

"No, you won't." Nathan scratched his head for a moment, looked at the large metal box and shook his head. "But then again, what else can fit a full-size person standing up that doesn't resemble a phone booth?"

"Exactly," Blake said. "What else do you expect me to do?"

Nathan walked to the door which made a hissing sound as it opened automatically. He greeted his father inside.

"Be careful what you touch," Blake said jokingly. "I don't want this thing to whisk you away."

"Oh, Dad. Really? Come on."

The push of each button made an annoying, awkward sound. The slide of each lever made an even more annoying sound.

"I think you're making a big mistake, Dad."

Blake ignored his son's comment and moved his hand along a plastic PVC pipe which concealed forty sets of color coded cables. Each set of cables contained eight sets of wires, and the wires at the other end split off into circuit boards of the same color.

"You're messing with the timeline, Dad. Don't say I didn't warn you."

"Yeah, yeah, I know. You already mentioned that." Blake disconnected one of the wires, and four blue lights went out. When he reconnected it, they immediately lit up. He disconnected another wire, and two green lights went out followed by a chime that sounded identical to an in-flight fasten seatbelt chime. He continued to disconnect each of wires while watching the indicator lights go off and come back on as he reconnected them. "Don't you want to see your mom again?"

There was no answer. "Nate?" Blake looked up to an empty room. He let out a huge sigh and continued to disconnect wires and watch the blinking lights while listening to specific sounds. He knew Nathan disapproved of this project from the start and to be quite frank, Blake was afraid of this becoming a reality. There was no way to know what to expect because the cameras he was sending into the past weren't broadcasting back to him.

After making a slight adjustment, he placed another mini camera on the floor of The Box and verified the time displayed on the control panel monitor. March 19, 2005, 3:00 P.M. He took a deep breath and pulled the lever. Another annoying sound filled The Box, then a pop, hiss, and a little bit of smoke appeared, which were all normal signs of success. Next was the bright flash of light, brighter than the past attempts. The camera was gone, and all that remained was an empty Box.

This time it was different. He sensed it. This time the flash was perfect. The pop and hiss sounds were crystal clear. With anticipation, he stared at the monitor, waiting patiently. An image started to form.

"Nate! Check it out! The camera went somewhere!"

He watched the monitor trying to decipher what the camera was displaying. "Nate? I need some help here, please!"

Nathan stood stone-faced in the doorway. "I don't like this one bit."

"Yes, yes, I know. Just come in here. What do you see?"

Nathan looked at the monitor. "I see… clouds? I can't tell. It looks like there's a lot of fog or mist."

Just then, a shadow-type image drifted across the monitor from left to right.

"Did you see that? Was that a bird? The shadow of a bird?"

"I don't know, Dad, it went by too quickly to tell. It could be. The camera may have been transported facing upwards. There's too much fog. I don't think this is the year 2005."

They both continued to watch for any signs of life when they heard what seemed to be an electric vehicle, judging by the high-pitched whir. The vehicle sounded as if was driving on gravel. A few seconds later a crunching sound was heard followed immediately by the monitor going blank.

"It worked! It had to work! The camera went into the past, and a car drove over it!"

"Dad, we don't know that. We have no idea where the camera went or what happened to it. You can't assume anything. The sky didn't look like that in the year 2005. Please, don't assume it made it safely."

"What else could have happened? The camera was transported into the past, facing upward toward the sky, just like you said. It probably was a very dull and dreary day. We caught a glimpse of a bird flying above, heard a car as it drove by, and that's how the camera got squashed. We have a gravel driveway, don't we? We heard the car drive over gravel, didn't we?"

"No, Dad, I'm not going to confirm that. It didn't sound like a car to me. We don't know when or where the camera transported. We don't know what we saw or heard, and we don't know what happened to it. You're assuming all of this because that's what you want to believe.

It could have exploded. Maybe that's what will happen to you if you transport yourself."

"No, it was a bird. I saw it. And it was a car. I heard it."

Nathan threw his hands up in the air. "I give up. Please, Dad, don't do this. Please." Nathan left the room almost in tears. Blake followed him until he reached the doorway. He shouted down the hall. "Look, Son, I'm very sorry, but this is going to happen. I miss your mom too much. The day that damn corrupt doctor caused her to die was the worst day of my life. I have to get her back. I'll be safe, I promise."

"No, you won't." Nathan stopped, turned around, and yelled back from down the hallway. "We don't know what it was that flew overhead. Maybe it transported to the prehistoric era. That bird you think you saw could have been a pterodactyl, and maybe a dinosaur stepped on the camera and crushed it.

"Oh, come on, a dinosaur that sounds like a car? Also, there were no cellular or wi-fi signals in prehistoric times. That's how this thing works. There's no way this could have been broadcasting from that period."

"Dad, that's not the point. That was an example. All I'm saying is those images could've been anything. Look, I give up. Please promise me you won't use this thing unless we have one hundred percent proof that it works."

Blake looked at his son but didn't respond. After a lengthy staring contest, Nathan turned

around and rushed out the front door, slamming
it hard behind him.

CHAPTER 2

"To me, it looks like the shadow of a bird."

Blake pointed his finger at Nathan who was playing a video game on his phone. "That's what I told him. And hear that? What does that sound like to you?"

"Umm…" Travis hesitated and looked at Nathan for the answer. When he didn't respond, he continued. "Well, I'm not sure. It has a unique whirring sound, but it definitely is motorized."

"Maybe a car?", Blake said with hope.

"Oh, no. I doubt that. I don't know what it is, but it's not a car."

Blake watched Nathan smirk at first, then shake his head in disgust and leave the room.

"Alright then, I'm probably just over excited that the camera made it there. What do you think, buddy? Do you approve of this project or am I getting in too deep?"

With slight hesitation, Travis responded "Well, I'm nervous, but yeah, I approve.

Travis went over and touched The Box. He ran his hand along the outer design. "This is truly incredible, man! You'll be able to see what the world will look like in one hundred years, a thousand years, or actually, see a real dinosaur if you go in the opposite direction."

"Now you sound like my son. The Box doesn't work from that time era. Either way, that's not why I've made this. All I want is my wife back.

Once I accomplish that, I'm not going to use it anymore."

"That's a load a crap and you know it. You're going to get addicted."

Blake knew Travis was right but didn't want to admit it.

Travis continued when there was no response. "Let me see if I have this right. When you use this thing, you can only transport to a date and time at the same location. You can't go to, say, Hawaii in 1902, or England in the year 2050. The Box can only appear at this exact spot at any given time. Right?"

"Yes, it's a time machine, Travis. Not a vehicle."

"Well, what if you travel a million years in the past and this location, at that time, was under water. Does that mean you'll drown?"

"Yes. But again, I'm only going to transport ten years ago, March 19th, at three P.M, give or take a few minutes. I'm not going prehistoric, or futuristic."

"Yeah, yeah, whatever," Travis replied. "And how do you get back?"

"The Box goes with me. I can either send just what's in The Box like I've been doing with the cameras, or the whole Box and contents. If I just send what's in The Box, that can't come back because there won't be a Box after it's transported. But if The Box goes too, then it can get back as well."

8

"And what if you see yourself from that time? Doesn't that disrupt the timeline?"

Blake couldn't get mad at his friend for all the questions. After all, he had to be just as worried as Nathan.

"That's only in the movies. I'm sure it'll be fine, but just to be safe, I'll stay away from myself."

"What if you transport with a fly in there with you? Will you merge like in that movie?"

Now Blake was becoming irritated and didn't answer the question – mainly because he didn't know for sure, but also because the questions were becoming more and more ridiculous. "Look, I'll have everything planned out. No need to worry."

"Okay, Buddy. I know I wouldn't have the balls to try what you're about to try."

"If you lost someone you loved as much as I loved my wife, you'd understand a bit better why I'm doing this."

"I guess so. What's there left to do?"

"I've tested it numerous times. That video we just watched was the first time the camera transported successfully. I just wanted your opinion as to what you thought we saw and heard. What I think is the camera was transported facing the sky, so I didn't know for sure where or when it went. Since then, I tried it three dozen times, and each attempt was successful." Blake brought up the video from the latest transport.

"Wow, that's pretty cool! You gained a few pounds since then," Travis said, tapping Blake's stomach.

They both watched the video of the ten-year-younger Blake looking directly into the camera, then placing it on a workbench."

"Funny thing is I now remember that incident when it happened back then. I remember not knowing where it came from and asked Sally about it. She said she had never seen it before, too. I didn't think about the incident since then because I probably took the camera back when I came to this timeline again, so I probably forgot all about it."

"Well, if you remember picking up the camera ten years ago and didn't know where it came from, yes, your time machine is going to work, or you wouldn't have remembered that. But then you've got to ask yourself - why isn't your wife still alive? If this is a success, wouldn't the future have already prevented her from her death? Are we in the same loop right now? Is there a future you and me or are we as far in the timeline as possible?"

Blake frowned. "I could have screwed up and was unsuccessful then."

"Well, why try again? Isn't it going to have the same results in an endless loop? Will the 'old us' be discussing this same situation in ten years?"

Blake scratched his head. All of this was starting to get confusing. "Possibly. But I can leave notes for myself this time."

"Who's to say you didn't do that last time? Do you remember any strange notes?"

"Come on already," Blake yelled, "I have to try something!"

"What if you said that ten years ago?" Blake didn't respond, and Travis quit talking. He knew when to shut up.

Blake transported another camera. They watched in anticipation. It was another success. The Blake from ten years ago looked directly into the camera for a few seconds and then placed it on his workbench. The screen went blank from when Blake, at that time, switched it off.

"How many cameras are on your desk at this point in time?"

"One, of course. I'm sending it back to the same moment. If I sent a second one a minute later, even a second later, there'd be more. I don't remember finding more than one camera, so I have to be careful and precise. I don't want to screw anything up."

"Fair enough, but you don't remember any notes?"

"No."

"Hey, let's send a camera one thousand years into the future. See what the world is like!"

"How many times do I have to repeat myself? I'm not doing that. I only made this for one purpose - to stop my wife from dying, and that's it!"

Travis frowned. "But how's it going to hurt anything?" Travis waited quite a while for a response. Blake wasn't budging.

"Sorry. So now what? If you stop your wife from dying, then that'll change the current timeline, won't it? Will we have even met? You did meet me because of your wife's death, you know."

"Since time travel doesn't exist yet, I have no idea what to expect. Life may continue the same, just with Sally in it."

"But I only met you because of Sally's death. You were depressed in a bar, and that's when we met each other."

"Dude, shut up," Blake said. Travis was asking too many questions. He saw the look on Travis's face. "I have no idea, but I have to try this."

Travis got up, ready to leave, and Blake gave his friend a hug. "Sorry about before. I didn't mean to get snippy. I just don't know what's going to come out of all this. I'm afraid, but I have to do this. We can let what we see in the movies ruin it for us, or we can just go with the flow. All this crap where the time traveler sees himself and things start to disappear from his life is fiction. It never really happened, so no one knows for sure. If I see myself from ten years ago, maybe we can go out for a drink and everything will be fine. It will just be another me with no side effects."

"I guess so. I'm starting not to like this."

"Things will be fine," Blake said reassuringly. "I think the big day will be tomorrow. Are you going to be here when I leave for the past?"

"I wouldn't miss it for the world. I'm worried about Nathan, too. He's pretty upset about this whole thing."

"He'll be fine. When he gets his mother back, we'll all be a happy family again."

"And what, his mom will just pop back into this world?"

Blake once again looked at Travis with the 'shut up' facial expression. "No, Travis, it'll be like it never happened. I think. I hope."

Blake gave him a firm handshake and a big hug again. When the door closed behind him, Blake sat there and thought about what he was about to do. *If I'm able to save my wife, should I even bother coming back to this time? Why not just stay there and continue my life as if nothing happened? Will I still be ten years older? Will The Box still remain since it hasn't been invented in that time yet? Will I be stranded?* He sent another camera and received the same positive results. "I'm coming for you, hun. I miss you."

CHAPTER 3

While Blake waited for Travis, he kept sending more cameras into the past. Buying them at a bulk rate discount was a great idea. So far more than twenty cameras were transported, but at that time, it was just one. Each attempt was a success. He tried other objects as well, just to be sure his device wasn't accustomed to only cameras. He even transported a rodent with a tiny camera strapped to its back. Something alive and with a heartbeat. The rodent scurried across the floor and entered a hole in the wall when the camera went blank.

Without knocking, Travis walked in and sat next to Blake. "Are you sure you want to do this?"

Blake just nodded. He didn't look like he was sure.

"What can we expect? After you zap out of here, how long will it take you to be back? When should we expect The Box and you to return?"

"It should be immediate. I'll go back in time, save my wife, and pop back at this exact moment. If all works the way it should, what you should see is The Box disappear and then reappear within a second or two, no matter how much time I spend in the past. That's hard to wrap your head around, isn't it?"

"You ain't kidding," Travis said. He walked over to The Box looked it over, not knowing a

14

defect even if he saw one. "So even if you spend five years there, it'll seem as if it's only seconds here."

"You got it," Blake said, slightly amazed at the logic of the scenario. "I can choose any date and time I want to come back, so I'll just come back at the same moment I left."

"I hope we'll still be friends. You'll know who I am when you get back, right? How will your wife get back?"

"Dude, I know this is a hard concept to grasp. Pay attention. Since I'm going to save her, she'd already be here."

"Why come back? If you can stop your wife from dying, why return here at all? Why not just live your life just as it is?"

"I've already thought about that. Please don't make this any more confusing than it already is. I don't know. Something is telling me I have to do it that way."

Another voice was heard at the front door, followed by a knock.

"In here, Nathan," shouted Blake.

Nathan walked into the room with red eyes from all the crying he was doing on his way over.

"I'll be back before you even know it." Blake inspected The Box one last time, hugged Nathan and fist-bumped Travis. He stepped inside The Box, programmed the date with shaky fingers, put his hand on the lever, ready to pull down.

"Are you ready?" Blake asked.

The Box

"No," responded Travis and Nathan simultaneously.

"Neither am I." Blake pulled the handle down. In an instant, The Box and Blake vanished.

*****

"Uh oh," Blake said when he finally opened his eyes. The Box was toppled over, slightly crushed, and too high up on a hill to reach. Blake must have fell out of The Box and rolled down this steep hill. The home he lived in ten years ago wasn't here, but this certainly isn't ten years ago.

"Oh no."

Blake was flat on his back, in pain, and was staring up at the purple-tinted sky. The fog was making it difficult to breathe.

"Oh no. No!"

Blake tried to crawl to The Box, but it seemed that more than just his arm was busted. He cried out in pain. Even if he could get to it, he couldn't possibly stand it upright. The hill was uneven. *Where the hell am I? When the hell am I?* He called out for anyone, or at this point, anything.

He was in a daze and kept losing focus. His vision blurred. That familiar whirring sound was heard traveling towards him, followed by voices. Although he couldn't make out what they were saying, he knew it was English and human. He felt a hand reach down and grab his arm. A warm, soothing hand. The pain vanished everywhere the hand touched. Then he felt as if he was floating. Yeah, there wasn't anything underneath him, but he felt himself gliding on air. *What the hell is going on?* When he was securely inside a contraption, Blake passed out.

CHAPTER 4

"We don't know who he is. He doesn't have an uplink."

"What? He has to have one."

"Look, Teresa, he doesn't. Feel free to check for yourself."

Teresa ran her fingers through Blake's hair to try and find the uplink in his skull.

"Think he's legit? The real deal?"

"It's impossible," Siri exclaimed. "Let him rest."

Siri and Teresa went about their business until they heard the mystery man with no energy speak softly.

"Where am I?" Blake's eyes fluttered. The light in the room was a God-awful green tint.

"Well, hello there. I'm Siri Bennet, and this is Teresa Davis. We found you on Cape Mound. Can you tell us your name? We can't find your uplink port."

Blake fully opened his eyes to take in his surroundings. *Uplink port?* Two visions of beauty stood before him.

Artwork by JellyEmily

"This isn't funny. Please, where's your uplink port?"

"I don't know what you're talking about. Where am I? What year is it?"

Siri looked at Teresa, Teresa frowned.

"What's your name?"

"Blake Stone. Where am I?"

"You're in our Skylab." Siri looked at Teresa again and spoke to her directly without opening her mouth. Teresa nodded her head and replied silently back to Siri. Blake saw this motion. "Did you say something to each other? What did you just tell her? What year is this, please?"

"2345, Blake."

Oh no.

"Where's The Box?"

"What Box, Blake?"

Oh no!

"My Box. The Box that was near me when you found me."

"We didn't see a Box, Blake. What's in The Box?"

"I was," screamed Blake. He was now in a panic. To get a glimpse out of the window, he quickly got up from the table that was hovering four feet from the ground.

Artwork by SPyWorkz from Deviantart.com

"My God! How many floors up are we?"

Teresa calmly walked to his side to catch him when was about to fall in five seconds. "Blake, you really shouldn't move so quickly."

"I'm fine!" Blake leaned over to look down even further at the strange city below. Just what Teresa prepared for, Blake fell into her arms.

"I don't feel so well."

"It's just nausea. You need to relax. You're perfectly healthy, inside and out. No broken bones."

Blake felt faint. "What's going on? Inside and out? You can see my insides?"

"Of course, Blake," Siri said. Just to see his reaction she added "We're Pshyres."

There was no reaction from Blake except a confused look. Siri guided him back to a stationary chair, one that was physically on the ground.

"Can you tell us more about yourself, Blake? What did you mean what year is it? What year did you think it was?"

"2005. March of 2005."

Siri spoke silently to Teresa again. They both laughed.

"Knock it off! That's just plain rude."

"Sorry, Blake. You mean to tell me you're from the year 2005?"

"No. 2016. I traveled back in time to 2005 to prevent my wife from dying. You mean to tell me that time travel still hasn't been invented yet? Even in 2345?"

"Uh, no. It hasn't. But you must be telling the truth. You don't have an uplink."

Now Blake was getting agitated. He was stuck three hundred and twenty-nine years in the future. The sky outside was green (he could have sworn it was purple when he first arrived). These people (are they even people) can communicate telepathically. They can see his insides. He was in a room that appeared to be thousands of feet above the ground, and he has no uplink, whatever the hell that is. All this information in just five minutes was too much to bear.

"What the hell is an uplink?"

Siri walked towards Blake and lifted her gorgeous, long flowing hair from the back of her neck. There it was, behind her ear - the uplink. A USB-type port built into her skull.

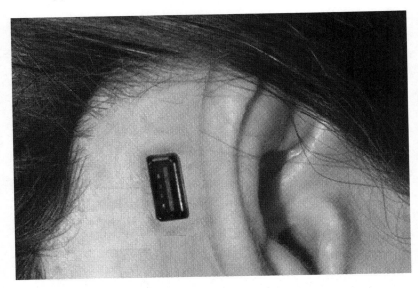

"My God," exclaimed Blake. "What the hell is that? Does everyone have that?"

"For the most part, yes, Blake. Everyone since the year 2100."

"What's it for? Are people born with it?"

Teresa covered her mouth to hide a laugh. It's not every day she ran across someone who never seen this before. She couldn't help but smile.

"So many things, Blake. You can plug in language packs to speak any language you want. Want to learn something? Just purchase that particular information pack. It also gives us real-time updates on our health, and that's only the beginning."

"Wow!" Blake stood there with his mouth open. He was only able to speak that one word. He was fascinated and couldn't wait to see what else this world had in store for him. Unfortunately, Travis was right. He definitely could become addicted to this time travel stuff. He kept staring at both of the lovely young beautiful women who stood before him. When they noticed, he apologized and looked around the room.

"I'm sorry." Blake finally closed his mouth. "I'm just in a state of shock and already have so many questions to ask. I don't even know where to start."

Teresa laughed and smiled a gorgeous smile at Blake. "I could imagine, Blake. I'm sure a lot has changed from over three hundred years ago."

Blake couldn't wait to get started to find out more but was worried about Nathan and Travis. Sure, when he got The Box repaired, he could pop back there at the same time he left, but not if he couldn't get back to where The Box was. *If I stay here for a week to fix it, would I be a week older? Would more than a week create problems? I hope it's not more than a day, let alone a week!* There were many unanswered questions about his world, too.

"I certainly want to learn more about your world, but I must get back to the location I was found, please. That Box is the only way I can make it home to my family."

"Our world?" Siri put her hand on Blake's arm. "Blake, this is still Earth, silly. Yes, we'll take you, but you really should rest first. Your blood pressure just went up."

Blake looked at his arm to see if he was hooked up to machinery. He wasn't. "I don't have time to rest. Can we go right now before someone takes The Box?"

"You were found on Cape Mound. That's an odd place to be. I don't think anyone would have any reason to take your Box. No one has been living there for over a century. The air quality isn't very good, so if we do go, we'd have to wear respirators because the fog makes it hard to see and breathe. It's a good thing our indicators went off and we rescued you when we did."

Fog? Blake thought about the first time the camera transported successfully. There was too much fog to see what it was that flew overhead. Then he remembered the vehicle sound. When the camera transported successfully for the first time, this is what he saw and heard. That must have been them coming to get him. Great, now he was concerned about the air quality surrounding his house in 2016.

"Respirators? You mean to tell me that over three hundred years in the future you still need respirators?"

"The fog is dense, Blake. Yes." They didn't take his comment as the insult that it was meant to be.

"I'd feel much better if I knew The Box was safe. Can we get it back here somehow? It's about eight feet tall by six feet wide."

"Yeah, we can have a Quadplane transport it. How much does it weigh?"

Blake frowned as he was ready to be turned down. "I don't know, eight hundred to a thousand pounds?"

"No problem."

Blake was now so very anxious to get started. Nathan and Travis would have to wait. It's not like he's going to be gone forever – to them it will seem instantaneous.

CHAPTER 5

"Here, take this." Siri handed Blake a flask of greenish liquid. He wondered if it was green because of the light coming from the window. "This will help with your blood pressure."

Without asking what it was, Blake drank most of it in one gulp. He looked at the remaining bit at the bottom of the flask and swished it around by shaking it in circles. "So, what's up with the green sun?"

"Oh, yeah, that's right. You didn't have filters back then." Siri knew she was going to have as much fun with Blake as he was going to with her. "It's still yellow. We just have a system in place that filters out the harmful rays the sun used to give out. That's where a lot of diseases came from," Siri lied. "The colors change throughout the day to help filter out all that stuff and also help with mood and emotions."

Again, Blake's mouth hung wide open. Wider than before. When they stepped into the elevator of this monstrous building, it fell open even wider because of the smooth descent of two thousand floors in just five seconds. Blake thought his jaw was going to lock open. Siri tried ever so hard to refrain from laughing at the poor guy.

Siri and Blake stepped off the elevator and into the street. Blake glanced back at the building he just exited, up into the sky.

Artwork by BorisMrdja from Deviantart.com

Siri pushed her hand gently under Blake's jaw to close his mouth. "You're going to catch flies."

It seems that old saying still held in 2345, even though the rest of the world had changed incredibly over the past few centuries.

As they approached a long tunnel entrance, Blake finally asked, "Where are we going?"

Artwork by Martaraff from Deviantart.com

"To the Quadplane. You wanted to get The
Box, right?" There was no response. Blake was
just in awe. They arrived at the first exit in the
tunnel and turned right. There it was - the
Quadplane. The biggest spacecraft type device
he had ever seen.

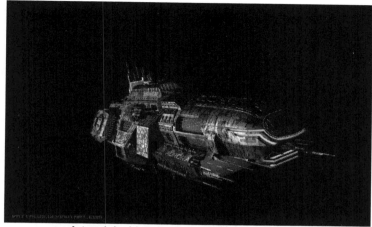

Artwork by Vattalus from Deviantart.com

"Can I drive?" Blake jokingly laughed.

Siri pushed a button on her hand-held remote which made it chirp as if an alarm was just shut off. The thrusters ignited, and all eight turbo engines shot out a huge hot blast of fire, followed by a cool blue flame, and then a steady quiet hum.

"Ready?" Siri asked. By the look in Blake's eyes, he was ready! The liftoff from the hanger was a picture-perfect scene right out of a Star Wars movie. It lifted so gently, turned slightly to the right, floating on air, and then blasted off at what seemed like warp speed but probably was just his imagination. Blake struggled from open mouth lock-jaw.

There were too many questions to ask and not enough time to ask them. The answers to those questions would only spark more questions. *How does this thing fly so smoothly? How fast does it go? What type of fuel does it use? How long does the fuel last? Does it use fuel? Are there bigger and faster models?* Instead, he just sat back and enjoyed the ride.

The flight to Cape Mound was over quicker than Blake thought it would be. He wanted to experience more of this awesome piece of machinery. According to the control panel, there was one minute before their arrival. Siri handed Blake a face mask. *At least this hasn't changed much in 329 years.* Blake took the mask without saying thank you and put it over his mouth. He didn't mean to be rude, he just forgot. *How long am I going to be in awe, every single day?*

The Box was visible from the Quadplane's window. "There it is! Do we get out here? How do we get my Box moved? I assume there's going to be a tractor beam that pulls it inside?" From this height, it didn't look very good. The Box was toppled over with its side caved in. Blake was paranoid.

"I know you probably have a trillion questions, and honestly, I don't mind answering whatever else you have. Ask whatever you want. I'd be doing the same thing if I were in your shoes." Blake smiled. He felt a bit better but knew it wasn't possible to ask every single question that he had on his mind.

"You have the mask on upside-down, Blake." *Guess it's not the same.* Blake re-adjusted his mask, Siri continued. "We don't get out of the

Quadplane, Blake. No need to. We're not going
lift it, so we stay right here while yes, what you
called the tractor-beam, pulls it inside. You may
want to peer out that window over there. Make
sure your mask stays secure when the garage
bay doors open, just in case."

Just in case what? Blake rushed to the
window and waited in anticipation. He danced
back and forth from one foot to the other, just
like kids dance when they need to go to the
bathroom, and stared out the window. Siri
couldn't help but laugh out loud. Blake heard the
chuckle and stopped dancing.

A loud mechanical garage bay door opening
sound was heard. Blake saw the tail end of the
gate fall to the ground, followed by a yellow light,
and then the dragging of The Box moving across
the land.

"Be careful! Slow down, please! Can't it be
levitated?"

As the box dragged along the ground, more
pieces started to break off. The scraping sound
was unbearable and even with the excitement of
the tractor beam in action, Blake couldn't watch
any longer. *You're damaging it even worse than
it is!* He trusted she knew what she was doing.

The hydraulic garage door sounded once
again when The Box was completely inside.
"Which way to the cargo bay? I need to inspect
it."

"Relax, Blake. Let's leave this area so we can remove our face masks. You'll have plenty of time to inspect it when we get back."

Blake stared out the window as the Quadplane took off once again. He tried to find any signs of where his home used to be. It was near impossible to pinpoint anything. So much had changed. He then noticed a brick outline of where a building once stood. *Was that my home?* Now there were more questions.

CHAPTER 6

"I'm sorry, Blake, I don't think those outdated parts are available anymore."

"Outdated?" Blake shouted. "I'll have you know these parts were way ahead of its time when I built this!"

Teresa put her hands up in surrender. "It may have been ahead of its time back then, Blake, but it's the year 2345 now. No disrespect to you, but those parts are now old. You might be able to find something on Ebay, but I doubt it."

Ebay? That can't possibly still be around, can it? I wonder if my username and password still work. What type of currency do they use now? What's the minimum wage? Do people even work for a living? Is a loaf of bread $800? Do they still eat bread? Blake felt sick to his stomach. All of this was too much to handle. Blake collapsed, but Teresa was already by his side as if she knew he was going to fall.

"You're not well. I already told you that you need sleep. Are you going to trust a Pshyre or not?"

There's that word again. Pshyre. Blake didn't ask. He was too overwhelmed with information already and too concerned about The Box. Either way, she was right, whatever a Pshyre is, he needed to rest.

"I don't have money for healthcare. Especially not in this world."

"There's no longer what you call healthcare, Blake. No need for it. The uplink catches defects way before problems get serious, so we don't need to repair ourselves."

Blake found it odd she referred to it as defects and repair. He was about to question her, but she continued right on talking. "We haven't used physical money since the year 2200 if you're referring to credit cards, bills or coins," said Teresa in a tone as if Blake should already know that. "We use fingerprint technology. Those who work have their earnings go into a highly secure account. When you pay for merchandise or services, you use your fingerprint."

"On a home computer? Shopping online? Don't people have a choice? They have to use their fingerprint?"

"Computers and online shopping have changed drastically too, Blake, but yes, you pay for everything with your fingerprint, regardless of what it is, how small or large of a price, and without an option."

"So... that means the government knows exactly how much everyone has in their accounts at all times?"

"Ah... The government. That's a topic we can discuss for an entire decade, Blake, but in a sense, yes."

"All my money is no good here? What am I going to do? I need to buy parts to get back home!"

"Blake, what you're going to do is rest, please. You'll have a heart attack if you don't." Teresa showed Blake the way his temporary room on the first floor, and without a single argument, he followed her. He wasn't going to question the heart attack thing or how she knew. He sat down on the bed and stared out the window.

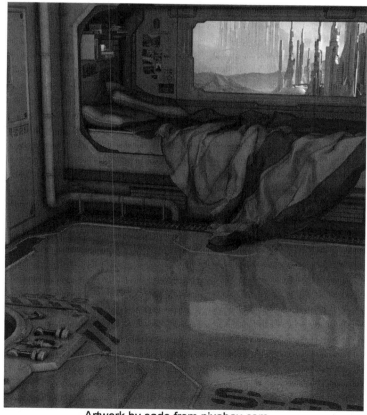

Artwork by sade from pixabay.com

What have I done?
Blake Stone fell asleep instantly.

*****

Blake woke feeling more refreshed than he ever had in his life. *Is it the air quality? The room I slept in? The bed I slept in?* The questions running through his mind wouldn't stop. He rested his feet on the floor and sat at the edge of the bed while his stomach started to grumble. As he walked across the floor, the sliding door made a woosh sound as it opened, just like in the Star Ship Enterprise. He couldn't wait to explore, but also couldn't wait to eat.

Siri greeted him from the corridor. "Hello, handsome," she said as he walked towards her. Blake didn't respond to her comment. *Is she hitting on me already? She's gorgeous, yes, but there's no way I'd be interested. I still miss my wife dearly.*

She changed her tune. "How'd you sleep?"

"Haven't slept like that for as long as I can remember. Is it something in the air?"

Siri smiled. "No, I mean, I don't think so."

Another audible grumble came from Blake's stomach. "I hate to ask, but do you have anything to eat? I'm starving."

Teresa looked at Siri, and then both of them looked at Blake. "Um, Blake, it may not be the same as what you used to eat. A lot of foods were found to cause…"

Blake put up his hand for her to stop. He didn't want to know. If they told him what was bad for him, when he made it back home, that would just spoil his enjoyment of eating.

Teresa scrolled through a listing of items on a transparent display monitor. It appeared as though she added something to an online shopping cart. Blake watched closely from where he was sitting. Yes, she was adding food to her cart from… Amazon? Teresa put her thumb on the fingerprint device and a pleasant chime sounded.

"Did you just order take-out from Amazon? Do they do food delivery now? Are they also a local restaurant?"

Blake was a bit disappointed that he'd have to wait for the delivery. He looked around the room for a refrigerator. *I need to eat something, just to curve my appetite.* He couldn't find one. His eyes wandered from wall to wall. There were at least ten unidentified items in this room alone. He went up to one of them and started to examine it a bit closer when he heard a doorbell.

Siri opened the door and grabbed the Amazon box. A sound from behind the door started to dissipate from whatever brought the delivery.

"Amazon has the drone thing perfected, don't they!"

The Box

Siri placed the meal in front of Blake. He stared at it, then at Teresa who was still smiling, then back at the plate. "Is this a joke?"

Teresa smiled and put her hand gently on Blake's wrist. *Is she hitting on me too?*

"No, Blake, it's not a joke. This is rapuce. It's delicious. Please, try it. I bet you won't be able to finish it."

"What? There's nothing to it. That won't even fill one tooth."

Teresa motioned with both hands to go ahead. Blake picked up the spoon, then put it down. *How the hell do you eat this? What is it? This has to be a joke.* He looked back at Teresa, who was still staring back at him. Siri was also staring. He picked up the rapuce, and bit into it.

38

Instantly a burst of flavor shot through his entire body. He felt a tingling sensation in parts of his body he hasn't felt a tingling in a long time. *Are both of them trying to seduce me?* He quickly shook those thoughts from his mind.

"Is it good?"

"Damn good! What's up with that tingling sensation," he asked outright.

"That's just the goodness running through your body. Energy. Go on, have another bite."

He wanted to, but he couldn't. From one bite of this magical food, he felt full.

"Don't want anymore, do you," Siri laughed, touching his arm and resting it there.

"Ok, you're right. I'm full." *Or is it that I'm anxious to get started on the repair?* "Can you lead me to the hanger where The Box is please?"

Both Teresa and Siri stood, then Siri sat back down. Teresa led Blake down the corridor and into the hangar. They arrived at The Box, which was now standing upright, the way it should be. How it got like that, Blake didn't know or care, but in its current position, it only accentuated the damage.

"I'll leave you to it, then. If you need me, just come the way we did to get here. It's just a left, and then straight."

Blake was anxious to get started and already was inside The Box, not paying any attention to Teresa, so she let him get to work.

CHAPTER 7

Two hours had passed without hearing a word from Blake. Siri and Teresa went to check on his progress. When they arrived, he was still working on the wiring and glanced up when they walked in. "I noticed you left tools for me. Thanks. I've used some of them, but others I have no idea what they are."

"How's the progress?"

"Slow. Although I'm able to power it on, it just doesn't seem to communicate properly. I think one of the boards fried. I'm hoping that's not the case. It's going to be impossible to find a replacement anywhere."

"What are the chances of rebuilding The Box with a modern board?"

"Slim to none. I don't know modern technology." He was so focused on his work that there was an uncomfortable silence.

"Okay, just let me know if you need anything." The silence remained, so Teresa left him work.

*****

Four more hours into the repair, Blake was losing his mind. He started to believe he'd be in the year 2345 forever, with two gorgeous women. *How bad can that be? Terrible*, he thought. *I miss my son already.* He struggled with more wires and resistors until he heard

footsteps down the hall. He glanced up
expecting to see Siri and Teresa but saw an
additional female.

Artwork by JellyEmily

"Blake, this is our friend Espy Vidot," Teresa said. "I thought you could use some help. She's the best electronics technician I know, and may be able to help fix your Box."

"You're kidding! Really? That's great, thank you!" *Are all women in the year 2345 this attractive?* Blake looked down at his clothes. They were a little wrinkled since that's what he wore to bed, but he didn't look too bad. *Do I? Does anyone notice or care for that matter? Should I care? I'm not here to impress anyone.* Blake went to shake her hand. *Do you still shake hands? Should I hug you?* Espy went right for the hug. *Are you reading my mind? Hello... Can you hear my thoughts?* Espy remained silent and stared at Blake. *Maybe not.* All three of them looked exceptionally gorgeous today and Blake felt a little out of place in his wrinkled clothes.

"So, you're the electronics expert? Even with this ancient technology?"

"It may be old technology, Blake, but, you've forgotten one thing." Espy pointed to the USB port in her head. "I've purchased an expensive electronics package."

"Even though this is my creation? Something like this wouldn't be in your programming, would it?"

"No, but it doesn't matter, Blake. I'm up for the challenge if you are."

*****

43

"Wow, this is amazing technology for the year 2016, Blake," Espy said while examining a circuit board she pulled from the over-flowing box. "Even for the year 2345 it's impressive."

All Blake could do was smile. *Are you hitting on me too, or are you just being sincere and polite?*

Espy smelled good. She looked good. He almost wished she wasn't there, trying to help, but he needed as much help as he could get. They both needed to be extremely thorough, taking their time with each and every circuit board. Blake couldn't focus. Here he was, trying to prevent his wife from dying, and he was getting turned on by Espy. He watched her examine each circuit board that he'd already inspected, looking for the same burned-out resistors or blown capacitors he had searched. If he missed seeing a leaky capacitor, she would probably catch it. Unless that is, she is just as distracted as he was. Maybe they should both look a second time when they finish the first round.

She glanced in his direction and saw him just sitting there, staring at her. She smiled and winked at him. Blake pretended he was looking at something beyond her and didn't respond to the wink. Instead, he picked up an already-examined board.

"You looked at that one already. We both did."

"Oh," Blake said. He stood up and went inside The Box so they wouldn't be sitting so close to each other. "Maybe the problem isn't the circuit boards. It's probably in the wiring. How about you continue looking at those boards, and I'll look at the wiring."

"Shouldn't we finish the boards first? You still have boxes you didn't look through. We're going to lose track of who looked at what. I think we make a great team the way we were doing it, don't you?" Espy said as she placed her examined circuit board in the completed box. There was no response. "We still have a lot of boards to go through. Are you sure you know how to put this all back together?"

Are you teasing me?

Blake was exhausted. He still didn't answer. He's been at this all day. The smell of Espy's perfume or whatever they wear these days was alluring. *You're probably doing this on purpose!*

Blake finally replied. "Of course I know how. I built the damn thing myself from scratch."

Before picking up another board, Espy stood up. "Okay. We should call it quits for tonight. You've been at this way too long today. We'll sleep in and work at this again tomorrow, okay?"

Are you saying we'll be sleeping in together?

"I'm sorry to put you through this, Espy. It must be boring searching every solder joint and testing each board."

"You're not putting me through anything. You didn't ask me to do this, I volunteered, remember? I want to help. I find this fascinating."

Again, no response. Blake was exhausted.

"You're too tired, Blake. I don't want you to miss something important. Call it quits?"

"Okay. I'll have Teresa call you tomorrow." Blake went for the hug since that's what Espy did last time, and she reciprocated. The hug felt more than just good.

CHAPTER 8

Blake, Teresa, and Siri sat there drinking their morning cup of coffee. Praise the Lord they still had coffee in 2345 and that it didn't cause any disease. *Or did it?* He looked in his coffee cup to find the answer.

"I hate to be a bother, but do you have anything else I could wear? I've been wearing the same clothes the past two days."

Siri and Teresa looked at each other with concern. Blake had no idea why, but he certainly noticed the look. "We'd be happy to get you new clothes, Blake. What size are you?"

Blake scrunched his eyebrows, scratched his forehead and gave them his size. Something didn't seem right. "I'm sorry, but I don't have a fingerprint account to pay for it."

"Don't worry, Blake. We got it covered. By the way, it's called a PIAA, Personalized Identification Access Account."

Even though Blake wanted to go with them to choose his clothing, he would feel strange asking. If they wanted him to go, they would've offered. *Or isn't how that works in the future?* He let it go. There were more important things to do.

"Can you call Espy, please? I certainly could use her help again."

"Sure thing," Teresa said. Blake watched in amazement as she tapped a few lines on her arm. Each tap made a different line glow bright blue. He looked at Siri. She had the same markings on her arm.

Artwork by JellyEmily

A few seconds later, different lines lit up red.

"OK, she said she's on her way over."

When Teresa saw Blake's reaction, she couldn't stop laughing.

Blake wished they would have discussed it first. He would've liked to have the new clothes before she came over. *Maybe it's a good thing. If I didn't look so damn attractive, Espy might stay away.*

"Thank you." He headed to the hangar to get a start on examining the rest of the circuit boards, and from there he'd continue onto the wiring. He stood in the doorway of the hangar and froze in place. *What the hell!?! Damn, damn, damn!*

The tall metal shelf containing the circuit boards was on its side. Blake carefully returned the heavy shelf to the original position but couldn't stop more boxes from falling. All the work that was done yesterday had to be redone. The completed boards were in a jumbled mess, mixed up with the untouched boards.

Just then Espy walked in, gasped, and rushed to Blake's side. "Oh no! What happened? Please tell me nothing's broken. Are you okay?"

"I have no idea. I just got here. Wonderful. None of these boards better be broken. I'll never be able to get a replacement."

Espy gently touched the palm of Blake's hand. There was that wonderful smell again.

"We'll get it done. I'll stay here as long as it takes, overnight if I have to."

Overnight? So much for Espy staying away.

Blake pulled his hand away and went over to the metal shelf for inspection. It looked just fine. How it fell over remained a mystery. *An earthquake? Are there still earthquakes in the year 2345?* He shook the shelf back and forth. It didn't even budge. They both started to box up the scattered circuit boards once again to begin the long, now even more tedious process.

*****

They both worked through the day. The only interruption that occurred was when Teresa and Siri checked on their progress, and bring him lunch. Blake watched Espy from the corner of his eye as she let down her hair by shaking her head. The way it flowed, it seemed like slow motion. She was the most gorgeous out of all of them, therefore was having great difficulty focusing.

"Last box, Blake. If the boards in this box are okay, I can help you with the wiring if you'd like."

They both continued inspecting each board when Espy commented. "Blake, I have to ask. Why so many boards? You know that most of these can be combined into a single board, right?"

Whatever attraction there was had completely vanished, and Blake became

51

defensive. "Yes, now, but not in the year 2016, Espy."

"Even in the year 2016, Blake. Look at these two for example..." She held up two similar boards, side by side, ready to explain, but Blake didn't even glance in her direction. She put the boards back in the box and realized what she'd done. "I'm sorry."

No response. Blake was waiting for her to finish inspecting a board so he could re-examine it. Blake gave Espy an exaggerated look and put his hand out so she can pass it to him. Espy handed it to Blake. "Really Blake, I'm sorry." She put a hand on his shoulder and Blake eased up, just a bit.

"Yes, Espy, there are a lot of boards. I designed it that way on purpose. Each board serves a special function. If I were to combine several into one and something failed, I wouldn't know the exact board to replace, now would I?"

"Makes sense," Espy commented, but she only said that to make ends with Blake. In the back of her mind, she had a much better way to rebuild The Box. If his statement were true, he'd know where the problem was already. Now that she saw how Blake reacted, she wasn't even going to suggest rebuilding it a different way.

They both finished the remaining boards just two hours later.

"Looks like none of the boards were cracked in the fall. No leaky capacitors. I know I've been very careful inspecting each one. It has to be something in the wiring, don't you think?"

All Blake did, at first, was shoot a look towards Espy. He couldn't hold a grudge for what she said earlier. After all, if it weren't for her, he wouldn't know for sure that all of the boards were in tip top shape. *Is she doing a thorough job?* It was best to have two sets of eyes examining them, and the only reason she came over was to help. *Is that the only reason?*

"Yeah, you're probably right. I hope you're right. Espy, I'm sorry about earlier. I'm too stressed right now. I'm stuck 329 years in the future and miss my son."

"I understand, Blake. I didn't take it to heart. I can help relieve some of that stress if you'd like."

Blake's eyes lit up, and his mouth dropped open but went unnoticed with his back turned.

"I'm a great masseuse," Espy said without a break in her stride.

Oh. Blake was happy that's what she meant, but also was disappointed at the same time. *Is that what she meant?*

"That's okay, I'll be fine," he said, fearful of what can happen. He didn't want to lose focus on his main purpose – preventing his wife's death.

"Okay, but if you change your mind, let me know. My fingers are magical."

If Espy was waiting for a reaction out of Blake, she didn't get one. He didn't let it show. *Can she sense my arousal?*

The Box

"I'd help you put everything back together, but you know best what goes where," Espy said. "Unless you do want my help, I don't mind."
He thought about it for a while before declining. He needed a break and to be alone. Once he finished putting it together, he might draw up a quick diagram of the wiring in case Espy wanted to help tomorrow. Blake got up and escorted Espy to the door before he changed his mind about her magical fingers. "See you tomorrow? Say nine a.m.?"

"See you then." Espy left Blake, walking the long corridor. He watched her from behind, not able to look away from the way she walked and her slender figure.

The desperation for knowledge about the year 2345 was growing, but so was the need to get back home. He was cooped up indoors all day, by choice, trying to get The Box repaired. *Why does the day seem to go by so incredibly fast? Is it because I'm busy?* If he had to guess, he'd say it was at least four hours earlier than what he thought it was. *Why am I so tired?*

Now his mind began to wander. What's it like out there? *Should I try to explore a bit tomorrow? Are flying cars finally invented? Was alien life form discovered? Did computers now operate at three million gigahertz with seven thousand gigs of ram? Is Microsoft still releasing versions of Windows? Does teleportation exist? Probably not, or we would've teleported to Cape Mound.* There are so many questions that need answering. Maybe he needed to experience them first hand.

He ran down the corridor after Espy.

"Wait! Espy!"

Right before the elevator door closed, it reopened. "I knew you'd change your mind."

"No, no... I've decided to take a break from work. Ever since I got here, I've been working to get The Box repaired. I need to take my mind off things a bit. I'd like to see what's out there. Possibly find an electronics shop, or do clothes shopping for myself. Or maybe..." He watched her reaction closely "I can take a car for a test drive."

Espy looked like she was afraid to answer, but after a slight hesitation, she made a stern statement. "That wouldn't be a good idea just yet, Blake. The roads have changed quite a bit since then. We drive much faster and fly much higher."

Wow! They do have flying cars!

"I know. I was joking." Blake found it strange that Espy had an extremely serious look on her face. "Sorry. Forget I asked."

"No, Blake, don't apologize. It's okay. If you want to go out and do something, then that's not a problem. I'll talk to the others about it."

The elevator door closed, and Blake watched it go down one thousand floors in the blink of an eye.

The Box

Artwork by CrLT from Deviantart.com

CHAPTER 9

Although Blake's new clothes felt more comfortable than any other he has even worn, it just wasn't his style. Neither were the colors. *I guess that's what men wear these days. What the heck kind of fabric is this?*

There were several different outfits to choose from, but none of them were very appealing. He made a choice, not knowing if it was the right one, and headed downstairs to yet another new voice coming from the living room.

"Looking sharp," Siri exclaimed. "Now you look… normal."

Blake glanced around the room for the new voice and found it instantly, coming from a very comfortable-looking recliner. Blake's eyes followed the slender figure from her gorgeous flowing hair down to her tiny feet. *Oh great, yet another gorgeous woman.*

Siri noticed Blake still focused on the new female in the room. "Oh, Blake, I'm sorry, this is April Paltrineri. A good friend of ours."

Artwork by JellyEmily

This was not fair at all. Not one bit. Each
female seemed more attractive than the

previous. What the hell is going on? *What a killer smile. What great big eyes!* Her walk over to him was even more attractive. Blake was afraid to get a hug, but he got one.

"Hello, Blake. Nice to meet you."

"Nice to meet you too." That's what was supposed to come out of his mouth, but what he said was "rice do neat you drew." Feeling a little embarrassed, he looked down at the floor. April smiled, turned around and sat down behind a table. She crossed her legs and patted the chair next to her. "Have a seat."

Blake carefully walked over to her and sat beside her. He looked at Teresa and Siri. They also looked more incredible than usual. Blake wondered why Espy wasn't there too, dressed even better she did yesterday.

Are they all trying to seduce me? He was starting to get a bit nervous but also aroused.

Siri walked up to Blake with a plate of something and placed it out in front of him. "Eat up, Blake. You must be hungry."

"Isn't there anything normal to eat? What about pizza? Cheese steak sandwiches? French Fries? A big greasy hamburger?"

"There's not many places that carry that type of food, Blake, not around here. They do in the secret city, but we'd have to travel across town to get to it. We call it the 'underground," said April.

"I don't want to know why it's forbidden, so please, don't even tell me. But yes, I would like some normal food, please."

"Just have this for now. We'll get you anything you want later."

The fork still rested on the table. Blake stared at the mystery food before him. He picked up his fork and poked at it. April laughed. "It's not going to bite, Blake, try it. You may like it better than that disgus... uh... hamburger you spoke of earlier."

Blake went for it. He stabbed the food, and without hesitation, put it in his mouth. He started to chew until he realized he didn't need to. It melted in his mouth. Blake's eyes lit up while everyone stared at him, smiling their gorgeous smiles. He thought for a moment that he was only there for everyone's enjoyment.

"You're all enjoying this, aren't you?" he said defensively.

"I'm sorry," Siri spoke up. "I have to admit this is remarkable for us. I mean, a man from the past comes into our time? Just think, how would you react if someone from the year 1687, 329 years before your time, came to you? Just think of all the differences between those years. Imagine what fun you'd have with that person. They didn't have phones, cars, electricity and so much more. They would be just as amazed, if not more than you are right now."

He placed the fork back down on the table and thought about that for a moment. "I guess you're right." He went to grab the mystery food with his fingers and got disgusted looks from everyone in the room, and then decided to use his fork again. "This is quite remarkable. I could live without pizza after all." He let it melt on his tongue. *Why doesn't it melt on my fingers? Why don't you have food in front of you? Did you already eat?*

"I was thinking, instead of repairing The Box today, can I go exploring with one of you lovely young ladies?" Blake was hoping for all three to be hooked onto his arm while he strutted around God knows where in search of God knows what, but knew that wouldn't be happening.

Concern flashed across the face of all three women. No one responded, just looks from one lady to the next. He continued "You know... an electronics shop if they still exist or for some more clothes, anything, just to get out."

April finally spoke. "Espy mentioned it to us yesterday. We can do that, sure. I'll be your guide and make a day of it. I'll show you around town. We'll see a film, go out to get some pizza, and go shopping." April had guilty eyes. Siri put her head down in her hands and shook her head. Blake noticed. *What the hell?*

"Why don't you go get ready? I'll finish cleaning up here and then we'll head out." April looked at the lines on her arm. "If we leave soon, we'll make it back before 5:32 p.m., the exact time the heavy rain will fall continuously for two hours and twenty-one minutes straight," she said with a laugh, knowing Blake would react to that comment.

He didn't. He was excited and worried at the same time. He picked up the last morsel of food with his fingers and tossed it in his mouth and headed to his room.

When he was out of earshot, Siri asked "So what do you think? What kind of readings are you picking up on Blake?"

"Well, he's very attracted to all of us. And according to his aura, he's also very nervous when we're all around him. What I pick up on the most is how desperate he is to get home. He's very vulnerable right now. From what I can sense, when the time comes, he will help us."

"Good work, April. Thank you. You came highly recommended, so we trust your judgment, but taking him out? I hope you know what you're doing," Siri said, trying not to offend April.

"Don't worry. I have it all planned out. When we see a film, it'll be dark. When we get pizza, it will be in the underground. While in the underground, we'll do the shopping. This way I can give him a full analysis and I should know exactly what to expect. While we're out, I think you should contact Espy. I need her to alter more of those circuit boards. It'll be more difficult to find the problem that way, just in case they decide to go over them again. Oh, and I'm also picking up that he has no idea The Box was dragged across the ground purposely, or that you tipped over the shelf."

"But we didn't even discuss that, how do you know?"

April seemed a little offended by that remark. "Yesterday you told me everything that happened over the phone, so I was able to tap

into his subconscious. Will you just trust me? He
doesn't suspect a thing."

CHAPTER 10

Blake had to look out the window of this strange vehicle everywhere he went. The ride was unbelievably smooth as if it was gliding on air. *Am I gliding on air? How the hell fast is this traveling?* There were so many questions to ask, and he already felt bad for asking the number of questions he did. He stared out the window gawking at the strange Tron-style motorcycles everywhere.

Artwork by rOEN911 from Deviantart.com

"I knew those would become a reality some day!" Even the lights around the wheels resembled the classic movie perfectly.

Things sped by them in streaks of light, and at the intersections, he wondered how there weren't any crashes, especially since there weren't any traffic lights. He looked up and got a glimpse of the flying vehicles in the sky. The traffic up there as just as busy as it was down here.

He also noticed a few people were riding true hoverboards down the street in lanes dedicate just for them. April was getting very nervous. *I hope he doesn't notice... I hope he doesn't notice.*

They finally made it to a huge hangar type building with a sign that displayed "Dome 3H – Ready." April rolled down the window and touched the biometric fingerprint reader. The doors of the hangar opened to reveal nothing inside except metal walls and lights that engulfed them.

Photo provided by ElioMotors.com

April smiled when she saw the puzzled look on Blake's face.

"Uh, okay," Blake said. "Parking garage?"

"Not quite." April flashed the lights and honked the horn. The lights around the car shut off, and immediately the entire environment changed. They were now in what appeared to be a modern city. Tall buildings surrounded the car and Blake watched the kids play in the street directly in front of them.

"What the hell? Was teleportation invented? Did we just teleport somewhere?"

April laughed out loud and didn't respond.

About 20 seconds later, gunfire came from the sky above. Blake jumped in his seat and looked through the sky roof. A huge UFO about two thousand feet long hovered above them. Blake's face turned pure white, but April was calm as could be. He felt the heat from above when this mysterious aircraft hovered above the car. He also felt the wind from the propulsion system. A laser shot out of the aircraft and crashed in front of the kids playing in the street. The kids screamed in fear and scrambled for cover. Blake also screamed "What the hell is going on! Why are you just sitting here? What is that?"

April laughed some more.

"Damn you, April, stop laughing at me! Please! You may think it's funny but come on already, enough is enough! What the hell is happening!"

April's face turned red with shame when she realized her mistake. "I'm sorry. I didn't think of how different this is for you." April flashed the lights and everything around them froze in place. The leaves on the trees stopped moving. A kid that was running from the horror floated in a mid-air stride. The sound from the spacecraft above stopped. Everything was completely silent and still. The fire burning that wasn't really burning didn't crackle.

"It's a 5D drive-in movie, Blake. I told you we were going to the movies."

"But movies weren't like this in 2016."

"I'm sorry. This is normal for me. I didn't even think of how it was for you. It's five dimensional because you can feel and smell things around you, too. Do you want to do something else? Is this too much for you?"

Blake let out a deep breath. "Now that I know it's a movie, I'll be ok. This is all too realistic and quite impressive," Blake said, staring at the kid who was floating from the mid-air stride, "but hang on..."

He stepped out of the vehicle and went up to one of the kids and tried to touch him, but of course his hand went right through. "Wow. Incredible. What happens if I walk down this road?"

"It's not a road, Blake. It's the movie surrounding you. Now if we went to a 6D film, you would be able to interact with everything around you and determine what the end of the movie will be by what you say and do. I just wanted to start you off with something easier."

"You thought this would be easy?" Blake sat back down. "Ok, let's continue the movie."

April flashed the lights and the world around them was once again animated. Throughout the entire movie, Blake kept ducking when things flew close above his head and even jumped when someone walked right next to the car door. At first, he thought it was a staff member of this movie theater coming to see if he was ok, but when he said hello to her, she didn't respond. April had to refrain from laughing now that Blake previously scalded her. She still felt bad about it and learned a valuable lesson - only laugh to herself.

CHAPTER 11

"That was incredible! What are we going to do now?"

"We're going to get that pizza you wanted. To the underground we go!"

"The Underground! Sounds dangerous. I hope the pizza is as good as it was in 2016."

"You are the only one in this entire world that will truly know that answer, Blake." Blake smiled because he knew she was right. He really would be the only one who would know for sure.

They drove for quite some time until they reached what seemed like a run-down part of town. It reminded Blake of a bad part of Brooklyn. "Are you sure this is safe?"

"It is if you know where to go. And I do."

They pulled into an alley, and Blake started to get paranoid.

Artwork provided by ElioMotors.com

"Don't worry," April said with a pleasant smile that eased Blake's fears. "I know where to go, who to talk to, what to do and say. Just follow my lead."

They exited the vehicle and walked to even a darker part of the city. When they reached the door at the end of the alley, April knocked. A small eye-level hole slid open revealing gorgeous eyes, staring at Blake, then April.

Oh no, another beautiful woman? A fingerprint device extended from the door and April touched it. Within a few seconds, the door made an electronic sound, unlocked, and opened. April and Blake entered.

"We're here for the pizza," Blake blurted out immediately. He was a little too excited. April gave Blake a 'shush' type of look.

"Come on, this way." Blake and April followed
this gorgeous female to a large room. The smell
of the pizza was just as Blake knew it to be.

"What'll it be?" said yet another beautiful
woman behind the counter. *How can there be
this many beautiful women in this world? Is
anyone just normal?*

April looked at Blake. She had no idea what
to ask for and counted on Blake's knowledge of
this forbidden food. Blake stumbled out his
words. "Slice of bacon and pepperoni pizza,
please. Extra cheese, mozzarella."

"Ok, um, that narrows it down to about sixty
different varieties. Can you be more specific?"

*Wasn't that specific enough? Why is this
woman staring oddly at me? Is it because I'm
ordering pizza when it's forbidden?*

Blake looked at April for assistance. April
tried to help as much as she could. "21st-century
pizza, please."

"Oh, the good stuff," she said, punching in
the order on another high-tech device Blake has
never seen. "Five minutes, we'll call you when
it's ready. Pay at the end of the counter, please."

The entire time Blake was at the counter, this
woman was staring right into Blake's eyes,
making eye contact, even while punching in the
order. Blake found this creepy and had to turn
away. He looked around the room. Even more
gorgeous women, despite the fact that they all
had USB ports in their head. *This isn't a bad
world to live in after all. Was the diet perfected?*

He kept his eyes wandering and saw a male. Average looking, as far as he could tell. *Is this the first male I've seen? I haven't been out much and not paying attention.*

The pizza tasted like a slice of heaven. Exactly like the pizza Blake knew and loved. April sat there watching him eat, and Blake pushed a slice towards April.

"Um, no thank you." She pushed it back.

Blake wondered why it was forbidden, but wasn't about to ask. He didn't want to ruin it for himself when he got back home. If he got back home. April showed concern every time Blake took a bite, and he tried to ignore it. He hasn't seen April eat anything since he arrived, and come to think of it, he didn't remember any of the women eating anything either. *That has to be why they are so thin.*

After the sixth slice, April looked as if she was going to vomit. She tried not to stare, and Blake had to turn away every time he took a bite. It was getting more and more difficult to eat with the faint gagging sounds she made which took away from the enjoyment considerably.

There were two slices left, but he had to leave them. The remaining slices were small cuts, and he could have easily eaten those too. "What's next? Shopping?"

"Sure," April said, glad to get out of there, "We'll shop right here in the underground."

CHAPTER 12

Blake was hoping to have a better shopping experience. Sure, there were quite a few new gadgets out – color changing clothes, skateboards that floated on air, TVs that were transparent when switched off, and remarkably realistic looking hologram sales people trying to sell everything under the green sun. Pet stores had new breeds of animals Blake has never imagined possible before.

Artwork by SkavenZverov from Deviantart.com

But he felt uncomfortable in this environment. It was too noisy. The music playing through the speaker system was nothing he had ever heard. To him, it was just noise. There were too many differences to comprehend. Too many people were staring, both men and women. *Why are they staring? Is it just my imagination? Do they know I'm from the past? Everything is too confusing. This isn't such a good idea.* He began to feel light-headed. At one point he nearly passed out. Once again, April knew this would happen and was there to catch his fall.

"Are you ok? Do you want to go home?"

"Yes, I want to go home. My home."

April held Blake's hand. "I know you do. We'll get you there."

Blake didn't know if he felt the way he did because of the atmosphere, the actual air quality, his surroundings, the people staring at him the entire time, or the amount of changes in 329 years. He didn't say another word.

"You want to go back to my place?"

Her wording made Blake hesitate.

"You know, your temporary home."

Blake was desperate to find an electronics shop since April volunteered to help purchase parts for The Box, but the possibilities were extremely slim. Technology changed substantially in his lifetime, and he was only thirty-eight years old. 329 years in the future was more than eight of his lifetimes combined.

"Yeah, this was a bad idea. I'm sorry."

"No need to apologize, Blake."

As they walked to the car, it started to rain. Blake looked at his watch. 5:31 p.m. Just like April mentioned it would at this exact moment. Just one minute later it started to downpour. He shook his head with amazement.

The Box

*****

April and Blake arrived back 'home' with Espy, Teresa, and Siri all sitting there, legs crossed.

"You two have fun?" Teresa asked Blake.

"Not as much as I thought I would. I'm highly impressed with the spot-on 21st-century pizza, but there were too many differences in your world. It gave me a headache."

April let out a laugh. "This is still Earth, Blake."

"You know what I mean."

Blake was exhausted but didn't want to be rude.

"Why don't you get some sleep? We'll all be here tomorrow to help you in any way you need."

Do I look tired? Does she know I'm tired? Just like she knew when I was going to faint?

"Yeah, I'm kind of tired. OK. I'll see you all tomorrow morning." Blake made his way to his room, thinking about several things. *Why isn't anyone else ever exhausted? Why doesn't anyone like to eat in front of me?*

He walked down the hallway and kept looking back at the gorgeous women. Damn, they were beautiful. All eyes were on him. He turned around and closed his door. *Something isn't right, and I'm going to figure out what's going on!*

*****

How is it that every morning when I wake up, I feel refreshed? It has to be my bed or the food they are feeding me. Which now come to think of it, I'm hungry again. He chose a new shirt and jeans and headed to the kitchen. Everyone was already awake and chatting quietly.

"Don't you ever go to sleep?"

"Good morning, sir. Those clothes look even better than the ones you had on yesterday."

Blake looked downward as if he forgotten what he put on. "Thank you." He paused and didn't look anyone directly. "I feel awkward about asking every day, but I don't know how to work the Amazon food ordering system. Even if I did, I wouldn't know what to order. Can I get something else to eat? Doesn't anyone own a fridge?"

No one answered Blake's last question, but this time, April got up and went over to the computer. "No problem at all, honestly, Blake," she said. Blake stood alongside her, excited to see the entire process. He stood a little too close, and April's hand brushed up against his leg. She didn't apologize.

"Oh, that looks good!"

"You don't want that, trust me."

"Well, how about that? That looks like it has loads of cheese. I love cheese."

"That's not cheese, Blake. Trust me. You don't want that either."

"Well what about that right there, A cheeseburger!"

"Wrong again, Blake. Look, do you want to do this or do you want me to help?"

"Sorry," Blake said, "Go ahead. I'll just watch if you don't mind."

April placed a few items in the shopping cart and pressed the order button. She touched the biometric reader with her index finger. A chime was heard confirming the order.

"Thank you, April."

Blake went to join the conversation with the others. In just a few minutes a commotion was heard at the front door.

"May I get it this time? I want to see who or what is delivering the food so fast."

"Go for it," Siri said.

Blake opened the front door.

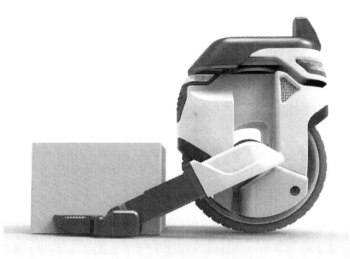

Artwork by Kobi Shikar

"It's a robot!"

The arms on the robot lifted the package off the padded seat and down to the floor. Once Blake took it, it drove away, automatically.

"That is the coolest thing ever! How did it arrive here so quickly?"

"It just does."

Blake opened the container. The food was nice and warm. Everything was still neat and in place. He no longer cared what food they ordered. Everything they've chosen for him so far was delicious. "I'm so sorry to have to ask you every time. And I'm so sorry that you have to pay for it. I'll find some way to repay you."

"Don't worry about it," Espy said.

Blake was almost able to finish the full meal, although this time he may have over-eaten. He left just a small amount on his plate. "Okay, well, I guess we better get on to the repair, what do you think? Who's with me?" He picked up his plate ready to put it in the sink. He turned left to right. *Huh? Where's the sink?*

Espy stood up immediately and looked at Siri, "I'll help you, Blake."

April, Siri, and Teresa remained silent. Siri grabbed the plate from Blake's hand. "I'll take care of that Blake, go on, go get your Box fixed."

Blake followed Espy to The Box, and when they were out of earshot, the rest of the women spoke amongst themselves.

"When do you plan on telling him, Siri?"

"And what am I supposed say? That I've been poking him with needles while he sleeps, taking blood work and injecting him with the good stuff?"

"You can't keep it from him much longer, April. He's going to notice the lack of men sooner or later."

"Not if he stays indoors from now on."

April stared at Siri. She wasn't done complaining yet.

"Amazon is going to notice that we're ordering food. Only humans eat food."

"You think they care? They're getting their share. They'll think we took a human into our home. That does happen, you know, Pshyres and humans living together. Stop being paranoid."

"Yeah, but it's extremely rare. What if Blake contracts the Blu virus as well?"

"Siri, please. I know what I'm doing. He's getting the injection every night at the same time I take blood samples. He won't get the Blu virus. He may feel very tired every day, but he'll never know it's because of the injections."

Siri placed a small amount of last night's blood sample in a metallic device along with the un-eaten food, and placed that into the uplink port of her skull and continued. "I need a full seven days of bloodwork. We can't take a chance and accidently kill off the rest of the human population. I want to be sure he's 100% virus-free before announcing to the world what we've discovered. Can you imagine how the human community is going to react? Just imagine - the world will be repopulated once again!"

April looked of fear. "I don't know if that's a good or bad thing, Siri. I'm a little concerned what's going to happen to us."

"Nothing. We'll live side by side in harmony like we have been."

"Technically we don't really live side by side. There are so few humans left I'd hardly consider that side by side. As for harmony, there's so few of them and so many of us, I'm not sure what's going to happen if it gets to a point where there are more humans than us."

"Listen, Teresa, we've been living among the humans for how many years now? The humans love us. It's just a shame that they can't love us the same way they love their female partners."

"Some of them love us, Siri. A lot of them still think we caused this virus when we first visited."

"I know. That's another reason why we need to fix this. We know we didn't cause it. If we give them a pure non-infected man to repopulate the human race, I'm hoping that will change the way the non-believers think."

Finally, Teresa spoke up. "What are the chances though? I mean, it almost seems impossible. Not a single male on this earth is capable of reproducing because of that damn Blu virus, and here, one just falls into our lap from 329 years ago. A perfectly young, non-infected human. Do you really think he's going to want to repopulate the world?"

"From what we've studied, men love sex. So yes, I do think he'll want to do this."

"And if he says he's not interested?"

"Well," Siri said sheepishly, "we can ask him to do an artificial insemination."

Teresa wasn't in a positive mood. "And if he still declines?"

"Then we keep sabotaging The Box like we have been until he co-operates. Trust me, eventually he will. He misses his kid and wants to get home more than anything."

"Does Espy already know how to repair The Box?" April questioned.

"Yes. But we're not saying anything until we know if he's a good candidate. If he's not, Espy will pretend she just found the solution, help him fix The Box and let him go home. If he is, then we'll ask for help."

"You just can't tell him if we don't get his sperm he's not going home. He'll know we've been using him."

A little green light lit up on Siri's arm telling her the blood analysis was complete. She removed the USB device and continued. "Why can't we say that? Sure, he'll be angry at us, but what other choice does he have?"

"He seems like such a nice guy. I'd probably feel bad for him if we had emotions like humans do."

CHAPTER 13

"What the hell?" Blake placed the circuit board down on the table.

Photo curtesy by Webandi from Pixabay.com

He picked up his magnifying glass and examined the board more closely. "This chip shouldn't be here. It's the wrong one – completely." Espy started to get concerned.

"I don't know what to tell you, Blake. I'm just looking for fried resistors or burnt-out boards. I don't know what chips are supposed to be there."

Blake eyed Espy suspiciously. "Technically this board shouldn't work with this chip in it. I don't think that's one of my chips."

He picked it back up and examined it a bit closer and continued. "I don't know. I guess it has to be. That could be what the problem is from the start. Maybe that's why I ended up here."

"You're the inventor, Blake. I'm sorry, I don't have the answer."

Blake removed the chip and inspected it. He looked at Espy. Espy tried not to look back by pretending she was examining another board. Blake continued once again. "That's very strange. Can we look on Amazon for correct chip? It's a standard 2-ohm chip. I'm sure they have it. We'll need to order one immediately if they do."

It was a good thing Espy sabotaged more than one board, which Blake completely missed when he put it in the good pile. She knew she was safe either way.

"No problem." Espy brought up the massive Amazon inventory and let Blake scroll through it, choosing whatever he wanted. Sure enough, it was available. Blake kept adding parts to the shopping cart. "I promise, Espy, one way or another I'm going to pay you back for all of this."

"We said don't worry about it, Blake. Get anything you desire. We need to get you home."

With ten different chips in his shopping cart and no idea if it was expensive or not since the total wasn't in dollars, Blake clicked the purchase button. He was sure at least one of them would work. The biometric fingerprint reader device lit up, waiting for approval. Espy walked over and touched it. The pleasant chime sounded once again. Blake rushed to the front door to wait for the drone. That's when Espy ran to Siri.

"He found one of the chips I swapped out! He knows his boards. He may find the others soon. How many days left before we know if he's a candidate?"

"As long as we keep feeding him what we have been, he'll be perfect breeding material in just two days. If he's not one hundred percent compatible, that might cause major problems. Even ninety-nine percent is dangerous."

"I know," Espy said, just as Blake came running past her with a package in his hand. She ran after Blake.

"I love this five-minute delivery thing! It's incredible!" Blake already had the chips out of the box spread out on the table. He tried to place one onto the circuit board. The pins on it were too large. He tried another. Perfect fit.

"Alright! There we go! Now I can start rebuilding! I'm sorry, I wish you could help. I don't want to be rude, but I need to focus. Do you mind leaving me alone?"

"Not at all. I understand." Espy left Blake alone to rebuild The Box, knowing damn well that it still wouldn't work.

*****

The power-up sounds coming from The Box was a blessing. It reverberated throughout the entire room. Espy came running in to investigate.

"You got it to work!" exclaimed Espy, knowing darn well that it didn't.

"No, it still doesn't work. It powers up just fine, but that's okay because now my diagnostic lights are finally working! This sequence of these flashing lights tells me exactly where the problem is! See? I told you having multiple boards is better!"

Espy gulped. *Uh oh.* Thinking quickly she replied, "Great, Blake! But before doing anything, please rest. You're going to have a stroke if you start this project now. Please."

"A stroke? From starting this tonight? How's that possible?" Blake thought about each time he fainted. Someone was there to catch his fall. They knew when his blood pressure rose. "Why would I have a stroke? Are you sure?"

"Trust me. You will. It would be from the excitement. Please, get some rest first."

Blake put down the tools he had in his hand. He stared at The Box for a full thirty seconds before giving in to his temptation. "Damn. Okay, how long do I need to rest?"

"I don't know how long, Blake, but I know it's at least a few hours."

As he sulked off to his room, Espy rushed off to Siri. "Bad news. He knows which boards the problems are in, Siri. I had to lie to him and tell him he'll have a stroke if he continues tonight. We don't have two more days. Whatever test results we have now will have to do."

"No. I will not risk the rest of the entire human population due to inconclusive results. You need to do something else to The Box while he's in his room."

"I can't do that either. What if that changes the outcome of the diagnostic lights? He'll know I altered something else."

"You're the electronics expert. That's why you were hired. I'm sure you'll figure it out."

Now it was Espy's turn to sulk. She went to The Box and stared at it like Blake did earlier. *What an amazing invention. What can I do to that won't cause suspicion?* Blake already knew that it powered on and the flashing light sequence told him which board had the problem. If she altered the wiring, he'd know that, too. Although she regretted doing it, she picked up one of the circuit boards with the intention to replace a resistor with a higher capacity one – knowing that when Blake turned it on, it would pop, frying a board. She hated the thought of doing that because if it fried the board too badly, she knew he'd never get home and it would be her fault.

With the board in hand, Espy started to remove a resistor just as she heard an "Ah-hem" sound at the door. Blake stood there with his hands on his hips.

CHAPTER 14

There they all sat – Teresa, Siri, Espy, April, and Blake.

"So… A stroke, eh?"

"Is that what gave it away?"

"Not really. It was the mystery chip that was on that circuit board. I know damn well I didn't put it there. Now will someone please explain to me what the hell is going on."

No one wanted to speak up, and technically, no one had to. Either Blake had to co-operate with them, or he wouldn't go home. Simple as that. He didn't know this but knew the odds were not in his favor.

"WHY ARE YOU KEEPING ME HERE," Blake demanded, pounding on the table which made everyone jump except Siri. Still, no one spoke for a few seconds. Everyone looked toward Siri to tell the story, so Siri finally spoke.

"Blake. Please understand that we have every intention of getting you back home. We just needed to stall you for a few more days."

"Why?"

"We are not who you think, Blake. We're Pshyres. We're not human. We've come from another planet to live with the people of Earth because our planet was deteriorating drastically more and more every day."

"Knock it off, Siri. I'm not stupid."

"No, I'm serious, Blake. We're what you call aliens. Why do you think we have uplink ports in our skull? Do you seriously think humans could ever have something like that?"

"Well, no, I guess not."

"And why do you think we're all... um, skinny and gorgeous. We run on software to talk, think, and act the way we do. Have you ever seen an unattractive Pshyre, err.... Female yet?"

"Come to think of it, no, I haven't."

"We're programmed to look any way we want, Blake. If we want to change our appearance, we simply purchase another software package. Here's what I looked like before my expensive upgrade." Siri displayed an image at the table they were sitting near.

Artwork by JellyEmily

"I like your improvement," Blake said shyly
and then quickly added "Umm, but you were
pretty here too. You still haven't answered my
question. Why are you trying to keep me here?"

"To save the human race, Blake. The human
population is at an all-time low because of an
airborne virus named Blu that hit back in the
year 2299. It spread so rapidly there was no
stopping it. Scientists think it was created in a
lab and released into the atmosphere by

accident. The virus traveled from air particle to air particle. With each air particle the virus attacked, it grew stronger and attacked more air particles. And since the air you breathe is everywhere, it kept getting stronger and spread like wildfire. The entire world, Blake!"

"Oh my god! How many deaths? What did the virus do?"

"That's the thing, Blake. There wasn't a single death from it. That's why no one caught on to what was happening until it was too late. The virus killed the reproductive chromosomes in every living male. Before anyone knew what was happening, humans were already doomed when they realized there weren't any more pregnancies. It was deemed the worst disaster in history."

"Worst? Well, yeah, that's obvious! But the entire earth? That's not possible! What about the pregnant people at the time?"

"It is possible, Blake. Not in the year 2016, but yes, in 2299, it was. As far as the pregnant people at that time, their children are the only people who remain now. But even they can't reproduce. It's all because of the air they breathed in. It went into their lungs and then spread throughout their body."

"Sounds like a terrorist attack! Did they catch the people who released it?"

"To this day, no one knows for sure where it originated. Some people think it was something alien related. We were blamed for about a decade."

"Am I in danger?" Blake said, covering his mouth as if that would change anything now.

"No. That's the real reason why there are sun filters in place. It shields out the bad air and prevents the last remaining humans from getting worse until we can find a solution. And now we have – you."

Blake didn't know if he was being lied to, or what the case may be, but this was unimaginable. "So, the human population is in desperate need of repair, and I'm the one to save it? How? Why can't you Pshyres mate with the humans?"

"We're created in a lab, Blake. That's why we don't eat or sleep. We don't need to. We don't have the female anatomy."

It was all starting to come together – slowly, but there were still way too many questions. Now was the time to keep going and ask them.

"Are all Pshyres female?"

"What you call female, yes. We have breasts, so by human standards, we're considered female, but we don't have the other female aspect. There's no need to, we don't have children."

"And you want me to impregnate a human female? I thought they can't give birth?"

"No, Blake, they can, but all the men in the world are sterile. That's why we need you."

The Box

Blake couldn't wrap his head around the concept that every single male in the entire world was sterile. He was sure they were just messing with him, but he kept on asking questions. "Is that why you took me to the underground? It's not a popular place to be, so there wasn't a lot of people there. You hoped I wouldn't notice the lack of men. Am I right? Come to think of it I did see a lot of women."

"Pshyres, Blake. You saw Pshyres. There's also a lack of human women, but it's more noticeable with men because there are plenty of Pshyres everywhere, which look like women."

"I'm not about to go out and have sex with women just to repopulate. I'm sorry, I have standards and decline your offer. I'm a tad irritated that you Pshyres have been sabotaging my equipment and lying to me the whole time." He turned towards Espy. "I would like you to repair it since you obviously know how. I need to go home. Now."

Blake stood up. No one else did.

"What are you waiting for? Please help me repair The Box so I can leave."

"Blake, you don't have to have sex with anyone. All we need is a sample so we can do an insemination, and then you can be on your way."

"Do you realize how long it's going to take to repopulate? Do you even know how long it takes for a woman to have a baby? And then that baby to have a baby of her own?"

94

"That's why insemination is the best way to go. We can inseminate multiple women at the same time, Blake."

"This is ridiculous!" Blake pounded his fist on the table again, making everyone jump, except Siri once again. "No. I'm not giving a deposit. I am not having hundreds of children. That may affect my timeline drastically, have you even thought about that? Now help me get home."

Again, no one stood up.

"You're holding me hostage until I co-operate?"

"I'm sorry, Blake. Unfortunately, yes."

The rage Blake felt was almost unbearable.

He glared at Espy and said "Fine. I don't need you. I already know which board the problem is in, thanks to my awesome idea of having multiple boards." He got up and stormed out of the room.

CHAPTER 15

The problem with the second board was found easily, thanks to his stupid idea, according to Espy, of having multiple boards. The power and hum of the equipment were such a beautiful sound. He placed an item of the future into The Box so he can send it back home and dissect it when he arrived, but the item never left. The Box made a hissing sound, followed by a puff of smoke. There were no lights indicating where the problem is this time.

"Espy, get the hell in here right now," he commanded. Espy arrived within seconds as if she was already waiting outside the door. "What the hell did you do to this? I demand you fix it right now."

Espy just stood there, looking downward. Blake knew he wasn't going to get anywhere by shouting out commands and demanding so he toned it down substantially. "Espy, look, I have no interest in repopulating the world. I need to get home to my family. You can understand that, can't you?"

"Unfortunately, no, Blake. We don't have those types of emotions. They caused too many problems. Our creators left that out of the programming."

"You've got to be kidding me. You must have emotions of some kind. I noticed you glanced down at the floor when I yelled at you just now. You must have felt bad at some point."

"No, we don't. We're programmed to react the way a human would. It made the humans easier to accept us on Earth."

"Can you please help me, Espy."

"Can you please help us, Blake."

It seemed there was no hope. Blake was to do what he was asked, or he'd never leave for home. *Or would I? Is this a test?*

"Please go away. Leave me alone."

Espy left, while Blake once again inspected each board. By himself. This time, with a fine-tooth comb. Now that he knew she could have replaced another chip, he had to examine everything again. What a mess. What a chore. His stomach began to rumble. Sure, he could use the Amazon ordering device, but he didn't have a fingerprint in the system. *What would happen if I tried?*

Blake went over to the strange computer and chose what was ordered last time since he knew he liked it. He clicked the order button. The machine made some beeps and boops, and out came the biometric device. He let out a deep breath and put his finger on the fingerprint scanner. "PIAA account not recognized," said the pleasant female voice, or was it a Pshyre voice. *Who knows anymore?*

He was stranded in the future without anything to eat and no way to get home. Ignoring the hunger pains, he continued his repair. *They can't hold me hostage here without food forever, can they? Without me, they can't repopulate the world.*

The rest of his day was spent inspecting everything over again, and it seemed like the process wasn't going so well. He kept losing his train of thought. *What if Espy continues to sabotage more boards while I sleep? What else has she done?* His couldn't let his anger get to him. He forced himself to focus.

A solid twenty hours later he finished but wasn't pleased with his results. *I had to miss something. I've been at this for twenty hours straight and it still doesn't work.* He knew every resistor, capacitor, and wire. Either Espy replaced one of them with an exact non-working replica, or he missed something else completely.

Would it be so bad if I co-operated? He began to wonder what harm it could do. *Maybe if I lie to them like they lied to me? I could tell them I'll help if they fix The Box, then get the hell out of here before giving a deposit.* He heard a noise at the door and turned quickly. A new tray of food was on the floor. His original plan was not to eat, just to show them that he's not giving in, but the food they were feeding him was probably designed to make him exceptionally hungry because he gave into his temptations rather quickly. He went over and started to eat without saying a word.

CHAPTER 16

Blake bolted away. *Oh no, how long have I been asleep?* The last thing he remembered was eating whatever it was they left for him last night. *Are they trying to drug me? Can they get whatever sample they need from me without being awake? He had no idea – it was the year 2345, anything was possible. But if it is possible, wouldn't they have already done that?*

Today was the inspection of the wiring. At least this wouldn't take as long unless something else was sabotaged. He felt hopeless. Once again food appeared at the doorway, but he left it untouched, knowing that he wouldn't be able to hold off too long.

*****

"What if he doesn't cooperate," April asked Siri.

"Oh, he will. He doesn't have a choice."

"Is his blood still a positive match for the human population?"

"Yes," Siri said while running more tests on his blood from last night. "I think it would be safe to say that we no longer need samples. All we need is a deposit, and we can get started."

The overhead monitors showed Blake working on The Box. "Poor guy," said Teresa, just because that was what she was programmed to say, not because she cared.

They watched Blake carefully as he replaced a cable.

"You were right. He found your faulty cable way too quickly. Too bad it isn't going to make a bit of a difference. I've altered his Box so that when he tries to leave, everything will seem like it's going to work, but nothing or no one is going anywhere."

All three Pshyres sat back, feet up, not a care in the world and watched Blake place everything back the way The Box should be. He set the time and date for a few seconds after he left the year 2016 and pulled the lever. The Box made every sound it should make. A few seconds later, the item was gone! Blake's mouth dropped open as he did a dance like no one danced before. He looked directly at the obvious hidden cameras and gave the middle finger.

Panic attack! Everyone dropped everything in their hands, and all three of them rushed to stop Blake.

Just as they got to him, he was inside The Box, hand on the lever. "Wait!" shouted Siri. "Blake, please, the human race needs you. If you leave now, they will be extinct. Please reconsider."

Blake hesitated. *Is it possible? Am I considering helping?* Espy saw Blake's fingers tightening on the lever. "Blake, please," she said, batting those beautiful eyelashes of hers.

"I'm sorry – I wish I never came here. I'm going to pretend this never happened." He pulled the lever.

*****

"Look, something appeared! What is it?" Only twenty seconds have passed since his father left. Nathan carefully examined the alien electronic device.

"No idea," Travis said, "but it appears that your father has made it safely. It's probably a gift for you."

Nathan grabbed the device and turned it over and over, looking for the on button. "It's not like my dad not to leave a note, though. Why didn't he come back with it? I hope everything's ok."

"I'm sure it is. He probably sent it to let us know he's arrived safely."

"But why just send that? It's nothing I have ever seen before, have you? And why couldn't he have popped back too, instead of sending this mystery device with no instructions? Something's wrong."

"Nothing's wrong, Nate. It's just a present for you."

"No, I know my Dad. He wouldn't do something like this."

"You're over analyzing, Nate. Calm down. I'm sure in another few seconds he'll pop back. Watch and see."

Nathan and Travis waited patiently. There it was, Nathan's dad fading in… and out… and in… and… out. Gone. Travis looked at Nate. "Um… You may be right."

CHAPTER 17

"What the hell! What did you do?"

"We did nothing, Blake. We're all standing right here. It appears your Box still doesn't work correctly."

"Bull. I sent an item back to my time. It worked perfectly."

Siri didn't answer. Instead, a blank stare came across her face.

"You're talking to someone telepathically, aren't you? What else did you do to my Box," Blake commanded, now more furious than ever.

One thing was certain - Siri's programming was spot-on! Her eyes squinted and then her mouth frowned. Blake knew she didn't feel any emotion what-so-ever. It seemed as if Pshyres weren't capable of dealing with conflicts because all Siri did was walk out of the room. Espy and Teresa stood there, gazing at nothing, or maybe speaking telepathically.

Blake stared at The Box. Obviously, he knew there was another problem, but he also knew he was closer than ever in figuring it out. He placed another small item in The Box and pulled the lever. Espy and Teresa jumped when The Box made a pop sound as the item disappeared.

"What else did you do to my Box, Espy!"

Espy did and said nothing. She had a stone-cold look on her face. Blake started to realize that her programming wasn't as great as he thought it was. Both Espy and Teresa left the room.

At least he knows it works, but now he has another impossible task at hand: figuring out why it's not working on him, but it is on non-human items.

*****

It was hopeless. Blake examined the board he thought may be causing the problem, but had no luck resolving the issue. He couldn't possibly go over the boards once again. This was too much to bear. Blake needed sleep. Pshyres don't sleep. *What am I supposed to do?* He didn't want to doze off for fear of someone altering something else. Before he became too tired, he created a simple electronic door alarm using parts from an unknown gadget he hated to break apart. If a door opened, an alarm would emit a high-pierced screech.

He got a whiff of the food that was left by the door. It was like he was in prison. That's what this was, technically. He was held here against his will. The only difference was there weren't any bars to slide the food through. He didn't touch the food on purpose. Was it drugged? *If I don't eat, I'd get sick, and they would get worried and…. Well, that won't work. Damn Pshyres don't have emotions.*

After a full 22 hours of trying to stay awake, Blake made a drastic mistake. He rested his eyes for just one minute. In that amount of time, he was out light a light.

*****

"So, explain what the hell happened, Espy. That was way too close. Why does it work on inanimate objects and not for him?"

"To be honest, I'm not sure. It shouldn't work at all. Maybe my alteration prevents large items from being transported? Maybe it prevents anything alive from being transported? At least I know what to repair when the time comes."

"I can't believe an expert like you made such a drastic mistake! He almost popped out of here, and it would've been all your fault."

"Yes, but he didn't make it out of here, now did he?"

The camera focused on Blake as he slept. Both of them studied his sleep patterns. "So now what are we going to do?"

"He'll give in sooner or later. We just have to wait."

*****

Blake's eyes bolted open. *Damn, I fell asleep again!* The first thing he did was check the door alarm. It was just the way he left it. He went over to The Box so he could get started once again and heard a light knock at the door. He ignored it. A few seconds later he smelled something delicious. He ignored that too, for about thirty seconds, until it was too great to bear. *There has to be something in this food to make me want to eat.* He opened the door setting off the forgotten alarm system, grabbed the food, and quickly slammed the door shut.

Teresa, April, Siri and Espy smiled as they watched the monitor when Blake took the first bite. As he ate, his realized he may be stuck there for life. *Is my food conditioned to make me change my mind?*

He took yet another bite. *What choice do I have? He took one more bite. Yeah, this food is poisoned.* He couldn't stop eating and knew the food was made to make you crave more.

"Okay, ladies, you got me."

Right on cue, Siri popped around the corner, pushing a device on wheels towards him.

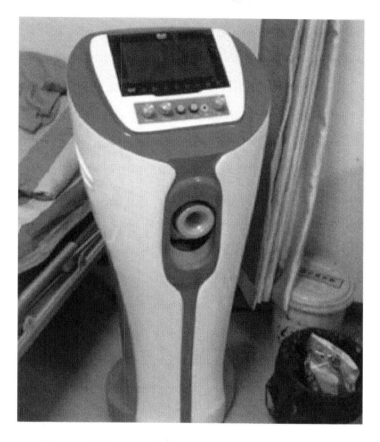

"Um.... No way."

Blake eyed the contraption with embarrassment. The video screen showed an online tutorial on how to use it, with pre-programmed movies if he needed help focusing on the task at hand.

"No," Blake said out loud. Once again, Siri just stared.

Siri shrugged. *Yup, this cold-hearted robot was emotionless.*

"It's the year 2345, and you don't have a better way to do this? This joke is not funny."

All Siri could do was shake her head no. She started to leave the room.

"I'm not putting my thing in that. You're going to be watching on camera, then upload it to YouTube to make fun of me."

"Blake, we don't care. We don't copulate, don't know what YouTube is, and have no interest in men."

She did have a point, but he didn't care either.

He was left all alone with just that machine. He walked over to it and viewed the video screen.

Instructions, Self-Help Videos, Start, and Stop. That's it. Simple enough. How hard can it be? No pun intended. He didn't need instructions. You put your thing in there and let the machine do the rest.

"No."

He walked away and sat down. The spying eyes of the young Pshyres behind the cameras were disappointed.

What choice do I have? I can't make Espy fix The Box. I don't have a fingerprint in the system to buy anything. I don't have any transportation to get anywhere. I don't know where anything is outside of this room. I can't even call for help. Is 9-1-1 still operating? If I escape, maybe I could find someone to help. The police? Is there even a need for officers? Would they believe me? Would they agree with them and force me to help repopulate the world? Maybe I can convince someone to help me by agreeing to take them anywhere they want in The Box – future or the past! Who wouldn't want to see the future? Who wouldn't want to see 2016? I can take them to any point in time. Even…. Wait a minute, the year 2299, when the disaster hit! I CAN PREVENT THIS FROM HAPPENING!!! Pshyres aren't too smart, are they? Why didn't they think of using The Box to go back to when it happened? I'd be willing to do that instead of having sex with this machine.

CHAPTER 18

"Siri, Espy, anyone... I have a solution!"

Siri came out of hiding almost immediately. "This is the only solution, Blake."

With confidence, Blake strode over to her side and got right to the point. "This disaster happened in the year 2299, correct?"

"Yes."

"And how long did it take to build the protection from the sun thingie?"

"You mean the filters? About fifteen years."

Siri smiled. She already knew where this was going. She ran over to Blake. Blake braced himself for impact as she jumped right at him and hugged him hard. "We can prevent this from happening! Why didn't I think about that earlier?"

You're not human. We're smarter than you.

"Only one problem, though," Blake said. "I don't think I can convince them. You know everything about this Blu disaster, I know nothing at all."

"I'll do it," Siri shouted. She seemed excited, even though it was impossible for her to be. "I'll go back and warn them."

He hoped this is what she was going to say. Blake smiled. *Yup, humans are smarter.*

"Here's what will happen," Blake said with authority, now feeling like he's the one in charge. "I'll just zap you to the year 2284. All you have to do is convince them to build the filters. Then you can zap back here to 2345 at the same time you left. As long as you implant that seed in their brains and they agree to do it, just leave."

Is Siri crying? You can't be. You don't have feelings. Ahhh, that programming thing again.
"You ok?"

"Yes, Blake, of course. It's a wonderful idea, but also very risky. If we travel into the past, wouldn't the problem already be corrected if it worked?"

"You sound like Travis," Blake said. "I don't know, Siri. You still don't have time travel in the year 2345. I don't know what to expect."

Without skipping a beat, Siri continued. "We correct everything in 2284 before it happens. With the blueprints already designed, it shouldn't even take fifteen years. When we get back here in 2345, if nothing's changed, we've failed. But if there are humans everywhere, we've succeeded. What happens if we fail?"

"Then I'll give a deposit," Blake said confidently. "But I'm not the one going. You are. I'm not sure what would happen if both of us went in that Box at the same time. When you're done, you can pop back."

"What if something happens and I screw the world up even worse?"

"How do you think I feel right now being here? It sounds to me like you're concerned. I thought you don't have feelings."

"I feel nothing, Blake. It's programming. I'm programmed to have every situation under

control and don't know how to react when I'm
not."

He wondered if Pshyres had some feelings
after all. "What do you say? Do you want to give
it a try?"

"Absolutely. I'll have to do research first,
Blake. A lot of research. Obviously, the person
who designed the filters is no longer with us. He
created it sixty years ago at the age of thirty and
passed away at eighty-seven. Next, I have to get
the blueprints on how it works, how to create it,
and how to install it. Then we have to go back to
the year 2284, actually 2282, just to be safe, and
meet the designer. Wow, that's going to be odd.
Bringing the blueprints back to the person who
designed it even before they designed it in the
first place."

Blake smiled. He knew how odd this whole
thing was. He's living it right now. Siri was on a
roll and continued. "We then have to convince
the humans that a disaster is going to take place
in just seventeen years and to install the filters in
preparation for it. I'm so sorry what we put you
through, Blake."

There was no acceptance of the apology. Not
even a nod. They could all go to hell for all he
cared. "Well, sounds like you have a lot of work
to do. Since you don't sleep, eat, procreate, or
anything, you should have plenty of time on your
hands." He motioned for her to leave. Pshyres
didn't have feelings, so he didn't care how he
treated her.

Siri left, unhurt, and started the research project. Blake wondered if he did the right thing. After all, he'd have to lend out The Box. *What other choice do I have?*

CHAPTER 19

It was the longest two weeks Blake ever had in his lifetime. He considered zapping Siri into the future just a few weeks and then back to the present time again to speed things up so he wouldn't have to wait for her to do all the research, but it was already complicated enough. He didn't mind that much. He kept busy doing a lot of research of his own. Not about how to fix the situation, that was up to Siri, but research on what happened in 2299. He discovered that the accusations against the Pshyres were horrible and disgusting. There was almost a civil war over it, and many Pshyres were killed. *So Pshyres do die.*

He also saw images of gadgets he wished he could bring back home with him. *Can I bring them home?* He also searched his home address and saw what the street he lived on looked like now.

Artwork by JoakimOlofsson from Deviantart.com

Unimaginable. That's Cape Mound, where they found me? No wonder why The Box toppled over. He continued to stare intently at the image. He didn't want to dig any deeper as to why it looked like this now, but he made a mental note to sell his home and move so his great great great great great great grandchildren wouldn't have a problem. *But then again, if I save the world from extinction, would this still happen to my hometown?* He didn't know how anything would affect the timeline. He didn't want to know too much, but he did add this to his printed collection of 3D photos.

"Ok, Blake, I have everything in I need. I found the blueprints on how the filters were installed, created, and work. I also know where the designer lived, and also where the computers need to be set up."

"Good job," Blake said politely. The past two weeks they've been getting along better simply because they had no choice.

"I even used Google to see what location The Box will appear when I arrive in 2282. Lucky for me, it's a wide-open field. What are the chances of that?"

"I'm so glad you remembered, Siri. I forgot all about that. That could've been a disaster!"

OK, so it's possible Pshyres are smarter.

"Well, let's get started. The sooner you get moving on this, the quicker I can get home. I hope the people of 2282 believe you or we're screwed."

"I've taken care of that, too. I have plenty of proof. Articles, images, stories, and more. When I meet the designer, he'll believe me. He'll know it's his work from the future. I found out that the filter is like a force field over the earth. It's all controlled by one hundred and forty-eight computers throughout the world, connected to each other via satellite that already exists in 2282." She handed part of her research to Blake.

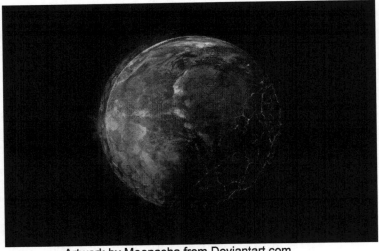

Artwork by Moonasha from Deviantart.com

"Wow, incredible," Blake said, looking at the image but had no idea what it meant. He just wanted to get home. "Over the whole Earth, eh?"

"Well, yeah, it has to be, Blake, since the Earth rotates," said Siri. Blake took it as sarcasm.

"I'm ready when you are. While you were playing around online, we had Espy repair The Box."

His eyes lit up, and Siri noticed.

"Now Blake, we realize you can just pop back home. We're not stupid." Blake wondered if she read his mind earlier.

"Please don't. We need your help, and if you think about it, this won't take any more of your time."

She was right. Once she left, in a few seconds, she'd be back. She could spend a full ten years there, who knows, who cares, it didn't matter. The fact that she can come back just a few seconds later no matter how much time she spent there was quite amazing, just like it would still seem seconds later to Nate and Travis when he got back home.

"Got everything you need?"

Siri opened the palm of her hand which contained a flash drive with thirty TB imprinted on it. In her other hand was a clear see-through device that resembled a laptop, probably to display whatever was on that flash drive. "I travel light."

"Remember, The Box will take you to an exact time, not exact place. You'll have to travel to get where you're going."

"Don't worry, I got it under control, Blake."

I'm not worried at all. I'm still mad at you.
"Okay, let's get this over with so I can get back home." Blake showed her how to use The Box. "You put your hand on this lever and when you're certain you're ready, just pull it down. I've already programmed in the date and time for you. When you're ready to come back, just lift the lever up."

If Pshyres didn't have feelings, it sure was amazing programming of their facial features. Siri put her hand on the lever. She moved her fingers up and down and grasped it tightly. She pulled the lever down, and she and The Box were gone.

*****

It worked! Siri was, hopefully, in the year 2282. Everything around her was completely different from 2345. *So this is what Cape Mound looked like before it became deserted.* She wondered what it looked like in 2016. The Box appeared exactly where Siri researched it would be. With great enthusiasm, she brought out her tracking device and with no time to waste, she made her way to the nearest rental facility. She could have chosen for the cheaper rental, but since she was going to save the world, may as well go all out.

"I'll take that one."

Artwork by Catetas from Deviantart.com

The slight hum of the vehicle was orgasmic, she assumed. She has never driven one with such power behind it, and to be honest, was a bit concerned. But that concern disappeared within a few minutes. Traveling at a mere 120 miles per hour - a third the speed of what this beast could achieve, she was on her way to see the designer, Steven Mason.

CHAPTER 20

Steven looked at Siri and wondered if she was on drugs. "Yes, I agree, this is my work. But come on, you expect me to believe that a disaster like this is going to happen? That you're 63 years from the future, and that you've met a man that's 329 years in the past?"

She pointed to the articles again. "Do you realize what's going to happen if this filter isn't in place?"

"Do you realize how ridiculous this sounds?"

Siri couldn't get mad. She has no emotions. "Do you realize what a hero you could be by doing this earlier instead of later?"

"Do you realize how long this is going to take to build?"

"Yes, fifteen years. No, wait, less than that. The fifteen years it took you in the year 2299 was also the development of it."

Steve looked at Siri suspiciously, then looked at her futuristic handheld device once again. He scrolled through the document for what seemed to be the eleventh time. "Siri, what's the real reason you're here? There's something you're hiding from me."

"I'm not hiding anything," Siri yelled. Once again, her programming was spot-on. "Look, all I can do is present this information to you. You can do what you want with it. Either way, keep in mind, you did build this thing. The choice is simple. Either you build it when it's too late like you did, or build it now and become even more of a hero."

"It's my work, that I'm sure of, but what if you're a terrorist? What if this does more harm than good? And if you are from the future, maybe this is meant for something else. Are you just trying to get me to build it now to change something to help you later? Maybe I only designed the blueprints and never really completed the project."

"Yes. I'm trying to change something later – to help save the human race!"

Steven glared at Siri and looked and then back at the futuristic tablet. "Can I keep this?"

"I don't know what it'll do to the timeline, but if it helps your decision, go right ahead. Don't waste too much time. Remember, the incident was said to happen on July 6th, 2299. It needs to be in place before then. Way before then. Please."

Siri left the room without much confidence. Steven sat there, looking over the documents. *I had to have created this.* He scanned every line of the diagram. *Did I really finish this project? Is there another reason for her wanting me to build this?*

*****

Siri stood inside The Box. What an amazing device this is. *I'm highly impressed.* She examined the controls, buttons, levers, and

121

switches. *Hm… I wonder. She carefully inspected the control panel. This seems easy enough to operate.* She ran her finger along the inside of The Box. *I wonder if he's going to do it ahead of time. Only one way to find out. I can make a quick stop to the year 2295, just to see, so I know if I have to convince him more. Blake probably won't let me go back a second time if I fail, so why take the risk of him not giving a deposit?* She programmed The Box for 2295. Without fear and just out of curiosity, she pulled the lever.

*****

Just one second after she left, Blake rushed to the window to see if anything changed. Immediately he noticed more men walking the streets.

"You've done it, Siri! You've done it!!" He glanced towards the empty location The Box once stood, waiting for the return. This whole thing should be immediate. She obviously convinced the designer to install the filters ahead of time, and now in the year 2345, it has prevented the human population from going extinct. He wondered how long it took her to convince him, and how long she's been there. He was still unable to comprehend this new time travel concept. *Has she decided to stay? It could be thirty years since she left but only thirty seconds for me.*

In any case, the fact that his Box wasn't back yet worried him. She should at least be kind enough to return The Box when she finished. If she saved the human race, that means she made it there safely. It also means she decided to stay, or else she'd be back already. *How much longer should I wait before I have to take drastic measures? The human race has returned, and the filters have to be in place for at least fifteen years.*

He was a bit angry with her not returning right away.

Then he dreaded the thought that his programming for the return date was wrong. *She's stranded there. It's my fault. But then again, she should be smart enough to change the date on her own. Maybe she's dead and can't come back?* He started to panic. He heard a commotion from the other side of the wall.

"Teresa? Espy? April?"

The commotion stopped, and Blake heard footsteps coming towards him. He rushed to meet the girls.

When they appeared around the corner, they let out a scream.

"Aaaahh! Who are you? How did you get in here?"

It wasn't the girls, but two other women. Both didn't have USB ports in their skulls. *Humans!* One of them immediately pushed a wall-mounted switch that he didn't remember being there before. *Did she just call the police?*

Blake backed up a bit. "Whoa, where's Teresa, Espy, and April?"

The two women looked at each other. "Who? There isn't anyone here by that name. Who are you and how'd you get in here?"

"I'm Blake. I've been living here the past month or so." He extended his hand to shake, but both women backed up. Blake saw the fear. "I'm not going to harm you, I swear."

"You still haven't answered our question. Why are you here?"

Blake realized the past had changed. *Oh my, Siri, what have you done?* He turned towards the two new women. "You wouldn't believe me if I told you."

"Then tell me," said a deep voice. Blake looked up to see a six-foot-six-inch man in a dark blue uniform. Apparently, the police were summoned by that switch on the wall, and they arrive quicker than the Amazon packages. There was a phaser-type device pointed directly at Blake.

"Whoa, whoa," Blake's hands went up immediately. The gorilla-sized man spoke with even a deeper voice. "Lea and Rose asked you a question. It's only polite to answer."

Before Blake responded, he looked over the ape from head to toe. No uplink port. All three of these people were human.

"This isn't going to be easy. Can we all have a seat and discuss it?"

CHAPTER 21

"This is Lea Gray and Rose Langdon," said the officer, introducing them like he knew them personally, but not introducing himself. The officer's nametag just read "Officer." A few things were already clear to Blake. Officers don't display their name for some reason, and there was no need for handcuffs in the year 2345. The intimidation alone of the police of 2345 was probably enough. Are all officers this large?

"Nice to meet you gals."

There was no response. They were waiting for him to explain himself and weren't there for chit-chat.

Without interruption, Blake explained the entire story from start to finish. How he was from the year 2016, The Box, the sabotage, the extinction of the humans, the Pshyres that were living here, and about sending of Siri into the past. All he got throughout his story were strange looks, rolling of the eyes, and nodding of the head.

"And that's my story. I can prove it. If I do, Siri wouldn't be able to come home ever again."

After a long moment of processing, "I believe you," said ape-man, "but you do need to go home."

"Don't you guys care? Did you hear what I said? She'd be stuck there forever!"

"From what you've explained it, if she hasn't come back yet, she's not going to, Blake."

"But what if she just has the wrong date programmed in for the return? What if she's in trouble? It's only been fifteen minutes."

"Blake," Lea spoke up. "You have to understand how this sounds to us. You said it yourself. If she could have made it back, she would have so by now. Sure, it's only fifteen minutes to you, but to her, she already saved the world. She would've come back right after she completed the task."

"She also could be dead," Rose said, regretting it immediately after it left her mouth.

"I don't know how it worked in 2016, Blake, but you need to prove yourself. You can't stay here."

The officer tapped his fingers on the table and just stared. Blake felt uncomfortable. He took out his ancient phone (to them) and brought up his app that summons The Box back, which was the reason he volunteered to let Siri go without giving her a hard time about it. He knew if he needed to, he could, but only if The Box wasn't damaged like it was when he first arrived. He dreaded the thought of doing it, but getting home was more important than anything right now. "I'm sorry, Siri."

Within a few seconds, The Box appeared, empty. Whenever or wherever Siri was, she was stuck there. For life.

There was no doubt now that he was telling the truth. "You happy now?"

"You're free to go."

Just like that? How could someone be so cold hearted as to what just happened? Are these creatures really human? Do they have emotions? Siri is stuck somewhere in time! Sure, the astonishment on their faces was priceless when The Box returned, but then for him just to say "You're free to go" almost immediately seemed like they wanted him out of here right now. He wondered if they knew something he didn't.

The officer motioned Blake to The Box. *Yup, they want me out of here.*

Blake shook his head in disgust, walked towards The Box and passed a table with a very cool looking gadget on it. He looked back at the officer, who was flirting with the girls. He looked back at the table, then again back at them. They still were not paying attention. He quickly grabbed the gadget and put it in his pocket.

He then stepped inside The Box. The guard and two women finally looked up and waved goodbye. *What the hell is going on?* Blake had to make a quick decision. Go back to Nathan and Travis? Go back and save his wife? Go find

Siri? He programmed a date and time into The Box, waved goodbye back, and pulled the lever up.

*****

"Damn, damn, damn!!!" shouted Blake. "Now where am I?"

Cars slowly drove past him. Fortunately, normal cars. Everyone was slowing down to see what was going on. Some started to take pictures. Twenty more feet to the right and he would've appeared in the middle of a highway instead of the back end of the Wilkes-Barre Mall parking lot. *What the hell? Why am I here?*

Then it dawned on him. The Box is not a vehicle. It's only a time travel device which teleports to the same location, just in the past or future. The very spot he is in now must be the room he was just in since they moved The Box from Cape Mound when he first arrived in 2345. *Damn! I didn't think about that!*

He brought out his cell phone and made a call.

"Hi, Dad! Are you calling from the year 2005? That is so cool! Did you see…"

"Nate, just listen to me," Blake interrupted. "This is important. I'm back in 2016. The Box is in the Wilkes-Barre mall parking lot. I have to get a crane to lift this thing onto a flatbed and bring it home. Then I have to figure out where to put it, because when I leave again, I have to make sure it arrives at a safe place."

"Leave again? Did something go wrong? Are you ok? How long were you gone? Why did it just teleport you there?"

"Yes, I'm ok. I left a month ago. I'll be home in a while to explain everything. Let Travis know I'm ok."

Nathan told Travis the news, and both of them decided to head out to the mall to find Blake. It wouldn't be too difficult to spot.

By the time they got there, Lane's Cranes was already on site, along with a few dozen people, recording the whole thing on their cell phones.

Bryan Kollar

Photo courtesy of Lanes Cranes

Nathan rushed up to his father for a hug, and so did Travis. Everything was under control. They all watched the crane lift The Box onto the flatbed. The entire process took about twenty minutes. In another twenty they were back home. Thirty more, The Box was unloaded into their backyard, not very far from where it was originally.

"Do I have a story to tell!"

131

CHAPTER 22

There they all sat. Blake told his entire amazing story. Nathan and Travis showed great enthusiasm the entire time and couldn't stop asking questions. Blake couldn't answer most of them simply because he didn't have the time to explore. He didn't know if the world was at peace. He didn't know who the president was, or if they still even had presidents. He didn't know if Donald Trump actually built the wall. He didn't know what video game systems there were, or if children still played video games. What he did know was that there were no children when he arrived, but there had to be children when he left, and he was pretty sure the world was saved.

Blake reached into his pocket and produced the toy gadget. "Here ya go, buddy. I have no idea what it does. I, um, found it."

Nate searched for the on/off switch. Nowhere to be found, just like the previous gadget. It looks real cool, Dad, but it's probably broken. It doesn't look complete. He placed it down on the table. In just two seconds, the bird began to speak. It repeated what Nate said, in a very clear non-electronic voice. "It looks real cool, Dad, but it's probably broken." The fluid beak movements and head turning were not that of machinery but like a real bird. Its eyes rolled back and forth as if it was examining them one at a time. Travis went to reach for it when it took

132

off. It hovered two feet above their reach and repeated the statement one more time. Nate tried to grab it right before it exited the open window, but it was too late. The bird flapped its wings and flew like a real bird, far, far into the distance.

Everyone except Blake laughed and laughed. "I wonder where it's going," Travis said. "Imagine the one who finds that thing. It's going to be on the cover of one of those weird news magazines. Bird from the future.

"That's not funny guys. That thing isn't supposed to exist yet." Blake watched it until it was completely out of his vision. He tried to hold back a laugh, but due to complete stress relief from being back home and everything he's been through, he burst out laughing - hard.

"So now what?" Travis asked.

"I'm not about to go chase it, are you? It's gone."

"No, no, I'm talking about The Box. I assume it's fixed since you made it back here safely but can you and will you try again? You know, to go back to 2005?"

"I'm not exactly sure what went wrong last time, guys. I'm a bit concerned."

"I think you should just call it quits, Dad. I told you this was a bad idea from the start."

I should listen to my son for a change.

"But your mom didn't have to die. I can stop it, I really can!"

"Dad," said Nathan, holding his father's arm gently to calm him down, "It's been ten years. Ten long years. You have to let it go."
Blake yanked his arm back. Travis looked at Blake as if he felt pity, which only angered him more.

"I can't. She was the best thing that ever happened to me."

"But this is too dangerous. Look, your first attempt nearly got you trapped in the future."

"First attempts usually fail. What's that saying? If you fail, try, try, again?"

"Not when it comes to time machines!"

A glazed look came over Blake's face.

There's no way I could back down now, can I? I already built the damn thing. It took me ten years to complete! I can't give up. I know it works, as long as I could figure out why it sent me into the future instead of the past. Once I figure that out, I'll stop the doctor appointment that went horribly wrong. It'll be simple. She won't go to the doctor that day. But then again, can I stop all the doctor appointments? If I pop back to 2005, will I know to stop the doctor appointment since technically it didn't happen? Or will my memory be erased from anything that didn't happen yet? Will The Box still be there because it wasn't invented or will it disintegrate? The bird I brought back with me still existed, but that may be because it already was invented from the time I was there.

Blake couldn't stop his mind from these impossible to answer questions.

But then again, if it does work, I don't even have to come back. If I do, would I have missed out on ten amazing years? I may as well just stay there. But then will there be two of me? How am I going to stop this when another me may still be there? What if the other me sees myself? Hm, how can I stop this from happening! I wish that doctor had never been born!

Blake's eyes opened wide. Oh my God. *That's what I have to do! I have to kill Dr. Baginski before he does the surgery that caused her to die! I can't risk trying to convince Sally not to go to the doctor only to have my other self change her mind back. But I'm no murderer, am I? Can I do it?*

He couldn't believe he was seriously considering this.

The more he thought about his wife's death, the angrier he became. It's at this point where Blake officially snapped.

Screw him. He doesn't deserve to live.

"Dad!" Nathan said for the seventeenth time, screaming it.

"Sorry, Nate, I have a lot on my mind."

CHAPTER 23

The obsession with Blake missing his wife was overpowering. He had spent all this time building the device for one purpose and one purpose only. To save Sally from the horribly-gone-wrong doctor appointment. He had no choice. In his mind, the only way to fix this was to murder Baginski. It's been ten years and he missed her more every day. If it wasn't easing up by now, it wasn't going to, even with the counseling years ago was no help.

The now anti-social Blake spent nearly a month, alone, working with The Box, nearly eighteen hours a day. Travis and Nate were upset with him because he refused to quit. Refused to spend any time outside the lab. If they only knew his new intent, they would sabotage The Box like Espy did. All Blake's free time was spent working with that damn invention. Blake had a beard for the first time, smelled due to the lack of showering, and take-out food containers stacked high. It was worth it! Blake found the problem - a simple software programming glitch!

Should I just leave? Should I even tell anyone? I can easily pop out and come back to this same moment without anyone ever noticing. All I'm going to get is flak from everyone.

He had put so much thought into this and was well prepared. There's no way anything was going to go wrong this time.

*****

He stood inside The Box. Frightened. *Can I really pull this off? Can I get away with murder?* He set the date of departure for the year 2004. He checked and double checked the programming. Everything was perfect. He checked his backpack. Gun. Check. Bullets. Check. Backup battery for The Box. Check. *That's all I need, isn't it?* Now he wished he had that gadget from the future. He'd send that into the past to see if it would survive, just like he's hoping his Box would. He became nervous and having second thoughts, but his hand still moved to the lever. *I have to do this. If I'm successful, wouldn't my wife already be with me? Have I tried this previously and failed?* Without thinking anymore into this for fear he'd change his mind, he pulled the lever. Poof. He and The Box were gone.

*****

There was no green sky, so he assumed his arrival was a success. He pre-set The Box to arrive back in 2016 at this exact time so he could make a quick getaway if needed. He closed The Box's door and locked it.

After a half hour walk through the woods and into the city, Blake rented a car and pulled onto

the street where Baginski's office was. He
waited in the coffee shop across the street and
kept an eye on the building.

The phone call he made previously asking if
he could speak with Baginski was the only proof
he needed that the doctor was in and was too
busy to come to the phone. When asked if he
wanted to leave a message, he simply hung up.

Blake began to sweat. He wondered if the
donut shop was wondering why he was sitting
here this long, staring across the street. He tried
not to stare, but he couldn't miss the doctor
leaving. After six long worrying hours and
nineteen cups of coffee later, Dr. Baginski
walked out of the office. Blake jolted up, but
then calmly walked to his car and followed him.
The entire trip he felt hatred for this man, which
was a good thing because now he was positive
he wanted to do this more than ever. He needed
to stay in this hateful mood, and just seeing
Baginski kept him angry. Blake's hands were
shaking. He wondered if the doctor noticed a
swerving car following him. After a twenty-
minute trip, Baginski pulled into his driveway.
While he switched off the engine and gathered
his belongings to take inside the house, Blake
cocked his loaded gun.

The doctor's door opened. One leg stepped
out onto the driveway. Then the other. The
doctor bent over and retrieved his work bag from
the front seat, and when he stood up to close
the door, Blake fired the gun. With a shaky

hand, the bullet missed the doctor and smashed the side window. The doctor dove to the pavement and looked directly at Blake. *Did he recognize me?* His facial expression showed he did, but that didn't stop Blake. He let off two more rounds, the first one hitting him in the arm and the second right between the eyes. Blake drove amazingly calm back to the car rental facility, but then started to freak out when he made his way to The Box.

What if I went to prison for this? When I get back to 2016, my wife would be alive, yes, but is it worth it if I'm in prison?

Blake stepped into the time machine. Now his mind began to race. *Oh no! I just thought of something else! There may be twelve missing years from my life. When I arrive in 2016, will I know what happened between those dates since I technically never lived them? All I know now is my life without her.*

Just then he heard sirens. *Damn! Too late now. No time to waste.* He pulled the lever.

EPILOGUE – TWO MONTHS LATER, BACK IN 2016

Blake kissed his wife softly on the cheek. "Goodnight, babes."

"Goodnight, hun. Don't forget you have a car appointment tomorrow to get the brakes checked," Sally reminded Blake again.

"I know," he responded. *Why can I remember simple things like a car appointment, but nothing at all from the past twelve years of my life?* Blake believed his wife when she said they were wonderful years, except back in 2012 when Nathan had a horrible accident on one of their family vacations, taking his life way too early. *Why don't I remember it happening? How can I not remember something that drastic? And this huge box out in my backyard. It's obviously a time machine because of the control panel, but why is it here and who built it? Where did it come from?* All Blake remembered was exiting from it. He believed that is the moment his memory was wiped. *Was it a gift from aliens? Did aliens wipe my memory? Did this device?*

Blake's new psychiatrist didn't have a reason for Blake's memory loss but continued to work with him on a weekly basis to try and retrieve the lost twelve years. Blake and Sally never mentioned the strange contraption to anyone, even though it may help determine why Blake lost all that time. Not knowing where it came from, word of this getting out could be dangerous.

Blake looked in Nathan's empty room once again. Plastered all over the walls were vacation photos and collectibles from when they all spent together as a family, although Blake had no idea where they photos were taken.

Blake opened the manila folder containing the documents of Nathan's death again. It was dated August 27, 2012.

Hmmm....

He looked out the window at the time machine, and then back at the dated document.

"Hun? Um... I have an idea."

Bio

When I'm not writing books, during the day I install and repair computer equipment throughout the Northeast PA area. At night, I package up orders from Ebay. My best selling item is Keurig Kcups. Over 100+ flavors to choose from! Check them out.

http://www.ebay.com/itm/131394908631
http://www.ebay.com/itm/131418807092
http://www.ebay.com/itm/131844070917

I also own my own business, designing websites and repair computers. Visit www.BryanKollar.com for more information. You may also leave me a message from there as well.